MARSCAR

The Scarllend War

By Jesse Calnan

EVA-MICHELLE
M
&FAMILY PUBLISHING

The idea for Marscar first came to life in 2013, during a conversation with my sister, Jasmine Berghout. We had planned to build this story together—me as the writer, and her as my creative guide and editor.

Tragically, Jasmine passed away shortly after we began. Heartbroken, I set the story aside, unsure if I would ever return to it.

Years later, in 2020, I found the strength to begin again. Over the next five years, I rewrote this manuscript twice, driven by memory, love, and a deep desire to complete what we started. With the support of an incredible publisher, I have finally brought the world of Marscar to life.

This book is written in loving memory of Jasmine Berghout and Joe Basciano (1927–2020)—two beautiful souls who have transcended this world but continue to shine light upon mine. Their spirit, wisdom, and kindness live on through every word and every page of this story.

CONTENTS

Crandrop
West Mountains
East Mountain
Majestic Forest
SCARLLEND
Castle
Shant Rock
Giants
Desert

"WHEN THE LAND REMEMBERS ITS
HEROES, EVEN THE FORGOTTEN
RISE AGAIN."

CHAPTER 1

arscar was a vast and magnificent land, a lost continent from millennia ago—filled with great beasts, strange creatures, brutal wars, and powerful magic.

Scarllend, one of its most storied regions, had a deep and complex history. It was declared a country following a vicious war over eight centuries before the events I am about to share. Before it became a kingdom, Scarllend was home to no man or woman. Only mystic beings roamed its terrain until its discovery by a lone human during the Great War.

The conflict was with the Volcanic Empire, a brutal nation buried deep within the eastern mountains, known as Volcanica. This territory, nestled just outside the original Scarllend border, was nearly impossible to reach. Fiery vortexes spiraled through the mountains, churning up and down, across and beneath the crust of the earth. The people of Volcanica were dreaded, gruesome creatures. Their flaming scalps were concealed beneath dark hoods, and flames burst constantly from their shoulders and backs—even through the burned patches of their heavy robes.

Their leader, Lord Blitzker, discovered a way to forge a portal that led directly into the unsuspecting Scarllend valley.

It was during this chaos that a brave traveler named Daniel Sable stumbled upon Scarllend. He had left the land of Slickton, which had once been home to humans until it became uninhabitable. An outcast farmer herding buffalo, Daniel eventually grew tired of the life he was living. He travelled north through mountains and even a great desert. In search of purpose and peace, he found instead a land engulfed in war.

After forming alliances with the locals, he found a way to gather the people of Slickton and brought them to this new land. Together, they formed a powerful army and joined the resistance against Volcanica. Their victory was hard-won, and Daniel Sable was crowned the first King of Scarllend. As king, he was fair and deeply committed to peace.

His first decree was the construction of a mighty castle to honour the brave souls who fought and fell in battle. This grand structure became known as the Memorial Kingdom. It stood as a lasting symbol of Scarllend's resilience and unity.

Over the next century, beings of all kinds came together to build the kingdom. Sable's Army, composed mostly of humans, settled in the western mountains. This uncharted region stretched endlessly into the distance. Many had tried to cross its unforgiving altitudes, but none had returned.

The castle and the outer walls of Scarllend were built at the base of these mountains. The Giants, who had played an instrumental role in the war, carried massive boulders to construct the stone gates. Another invaluable ally was the

Burrowers, creatures with powerful digging abilities. They helped create a vast tunnel system that cut through the mountains and opened paths to many regions. These creatures made the tunnels their permanent home and continued to expand their subterranean world.

With the help of the Burrowers and the powerful magic of the Gnomes, the great tunnel was completed after centuries of work.

Following Daniel Sable's death, Scarllend flourished. Four centuries later, it had grown into a powerful nation that was peaceful and prosperous, with thriving villages, fertile farmland, and dense forests.

As the population increased, many people moved within the castle walls. Eventually, a second kingdom was established beneath the eastern mountains. A smaller castle and surrounding villages formed a new region known as Shantrock. The Duke of Shantrock, descended from the Sable bloodline, governed this land, while the King of Scarllend ruled the west.

Together, the two rulers—bound by family and tradition—maintained peace and unity across Scarllend. However, this harmony came to an end in the Era of the 400s.

Two brothers were born into the royal family. The eldest received the throne, while the youngest was named Duke of Shantrock. Resentful of his position, the younger brother rebelled. Gathering his forces, he launched an attack that sparked a war lasting over four hundred years.

What began as a brutal onslaught turned into a long standoff. Shantrock declared independence, and although outright war ceased, cold tensions continued. Armies remained stationed at the borders, and Shantrock became infamous for its sneak attacks.

Meanwhile, Scarllend faced internal conflicts. It struggled to maintain peace with the Leprechauns of the far forest, who were often at odds with the Gnomes. The new Lord of Shantrock made deals with the Leprechauns, using them as spies and invaders, which further destabilized the region.

The stalemate finally ended when the Duke of Shantrock was betrayed and murdered by his own head of the military, Lord Diablo. Seizing power, Diablo reignited the war, recruiting Orcs and Ogres from the mountain tribes to launch a full-scale invasion.

Caught off guard, Scarllend struggled to defend itself. Many eastern towns fell quickly to Shantrock's forces. Despite the nation's vastness, Scarllend lacked the military strength and strategic coordination needed to hold its ground.

Now, as new forces rise and ancient powers stir once more, the fate of Scarllend—and of Marscar itself—hangs in the balance.

The new king of Scarllend was then Francis Sable, a weak and indecisive man. He had never truly prepared for an uprising. Though a small army was scattered throughout the country, his strongest forces remained stationed at the gates of the Memorial Kingdom. Shantrock had managed to build a nearby base, and ongoing battles at the castle gates had become all too common.

One dreadful, smoke-filled evening, a brutal battle erupted at the base of Mount Scarllend, beneath the towering kingdom. The Shantrock army was pushing to gain ground by forcing their way into the mountain region. The soldiers of Scarllend, familiar with the terrain, used the strategic height and valley contours to defend their position—until one night. That night offered no tactics, only chaos. Only blood.

Commander Shorpal, chief of the Scarllend military, led his men into the fray. His presence on the battlefield was commanding. Riding a tall black horse, sword spinning in wide arcs, he drove back the enemy with relentless force. For a moment, it looked as though Scarllend would hold the line.

But amidst the clash, a Shantrock soldier slipped through the chaos. He lunged upward, grabbed Shorpal by the leg, and yanked him from the saddle. As they both fell, the attacker drove a razor-sharp blade into Shorpal's chest. The steel sliced through his armor with sickening ease. Blood poured from the wound as the commander hit the ground, lifeless.

A few paces away, a great knight named Ryker witnessed the tragedy. From atop his horse, he saw Shorpal's final moment. Rage overtook him. As the assassin tried to retreat, Ryker charged through the chaos, shoving past friend and foe alike. With a mighty leap and precise aim, he buried his sword into the killer's back.

But as victory pulsed in his veins, a heavy fog clouded Ryker's mind. The image of his fallen friend haunted him, threatening to overwhelm his senses. For a moment, grief seized him. Then, resolve returned. He turned his steed toward the great natural staircase leading up to the kingdom and galloped away.

Atop the wall, two towers flanked a colossal gate. A small civilian door at the base of the stone wall opened just in time. Ryker burst through the courtyard, racing toward the king's tower. The castle, carved from the very mountain it stood on, loomed above him—a silent witness to centuries of struggle.

He entered the tower and ascended a dim stone stairwell. At the top stood a golden door, guarded by two men wielding battle axes. Recognizing Ryker's rank, they bowed and stepped aside. Ryker pressed a protruding stone in the wall, triggering a mechanism that slid the doors open.

Inside, the royal chamber glowed with soft candlelight.

Velvet carpet lined the floor, and the walls bore paintings of Scarllend's past kings and breathtaking landscapes. Twin spiral staircases framed a grand window, where a man in a dark purple gown stood, his jeweled crown glittering. He was King Francis Sable, ruler of Scarllend.

The king turned slowly. Below, the battle raged on.

"What is the report, Sir Ryker?" he asked solemnly.

Ryker stood tall and answered, "Shorpal is dead, my lord."

The king gasped, clutching his chest and stumbling back. Ryker rushed forward, but Francis waved him off and straightened himself.

"How can this be?" he demanded, eyes wide.

"He was taken in battle. I avenged him," Ryker replied, his voice heavy with pain.

The king's expression darkened. "This is madness. The commander-in-chief is dead!"

Ryker hesitated, then spoke. "Who do you plan on appointing, sire? I can hold a tryout or assist with choosing someone."

Francis shook his head slowly. "That will not be necessary. The new commander-in-chief stands before me."

Ryker looked around, startled. "Are you certain, my lord?"

"Yes. And I already have a task for you. The Shantrock army grows stronger each week. They take our towns and recruit from our people. They now control a long stretch from their castle to our borders. It is time we act."

He pointed toward the northern region on a worn map beside him.

"The north has yet to fall. Towns near the Majestic Forest and the city of Crandrop remain untouched. Crandrop has a private army. They have held off the Orcs from the northwest and protected their land. We need their strength. Seek out allies among the forest beings too. They may still honour old pacts."

Ryker nodded with growing determination.

"Your first command is to ride north. Unite those who will fight. Bring them back, and we will take the valley."

"Yes, my lord." Ryker bowed deeply, then left without another word.

He descended the castle steps, his thoughts racing. He needed to pack—and to say goodbye.

His quarters were on the next floor down. There, his pregnant wife, Petunia, awaited. She was close to delivering their child, and worry had carved shadows beneath her eyes.

"You are leaving again, are you not?" she asked softly as he entered.

"I must. The king has given me a mission—"

"You are all I have, Ryker," she whispered, tears glistening. "Do not make me raise this child alone."

He stepped forward, holding her close. "I will return. I promise."

Petunia wiped her eyes and stood tall. "Then go. The kingdom needs you. Our child will need you too. I hope you remember that. I will be thinking of you every moment you are away. I truly hope you will do the same."

They held each other tightly. Ryker gave her a tender kiss. After a strong, heartfelt moment, he turned and walked away. Petunia wept silently as he left. But before he could go, she softly called his name. When he turned back, she handed him a purple handkerchief.

"Keep this with you," she said. "Wear it on your arm. Let it remind you of me."

Ryker took the handkerchief and nodded solemnly. He left the room carrying a deep sorrow and descended the stairway with a sinking feeling that he might never see it again.

As he walked, doubt crept into his mind. Who was he to run an army? He did not feel worthy of the title. He did not think he would ever be the knight that Shorpal was. What bothered him most, though, was the thought of leaving the only woman he had ever loved—his poor wife, Petunia—to care for their child alone.

Still, he convinced himself it was the right decision. He needed to unite the country so that his child could live in a land that was free.

The burden weighed on him all the way to the stables. There, Ryker found a young squire preparing to remove the gear from his black horse.

"Stop what you are doing," Ryker ordered. "I need that horse." The squire obeyed without question.

"Have you seen much battle?" Ryker asked as he fastened his pack.

"Not much, sir," the boy replied.

"Would you like to come on a quest?" Ryker asked with a half-smile.

"Seriously? What kind of quest?"

"You will find out along the way. Saddle up."

The squire hesitated. "I was supposed to do chores..."

"Your new chore is serving your commander on a vital mission."

"Well heck, anything to get out of this place. I have been dreaming of an adventure my entire life."

As they readied the gear, a loud voice interrupted.

"Hey! That is my squire. Squire Billy. You are not taking him."

A burly knight strode over, frowning. He was known as a rough man, not to be messed with.

And you are?" Ryker asked.

"Sir Derk, and I need him to prep my weapons. He will not be going anywhere."

"Then come with us. I am going to Crandrop, north of the Majestic Forest."

Derk raised an eyebrow. "Well, I have never been that far north before. It might actually be fun. Count us in."

"Good," Ryker replied. "We will ride through the Mountain Tunnel. It is an old path built by the Burrowers."

The three mounted up, each armed with a bow, sword, axe, and dagger. They passed through the courtyard and entered a hidden tunnel beneath the castle. The path twisted for miles until they reached a stairwell and a solid stone door.

Ryker pulled out a slender key and slid it into a crack. With a deep groan, the stone door split and lowered into the ground.

Behind it, the ancient Burrowers' tunnel yawned before them, leading deep into the unknown north.

CHAPTER 3

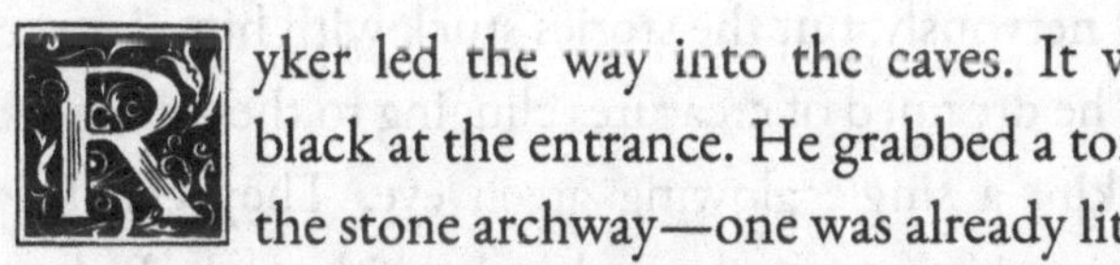

Ryker led the way into the caves. It was nearly pitch black at the entrance. He grabbed a torch mounted on the stone archway—one was already lit outside, and a bundle of unlit ones rested just inside. He struck the flames and handed a torch each to Derk and Billy.

As they ventured deeper, the darkness gave way to a surprisingly manicured passage. Candle holders lined the stone walls, and when Ryker lit one, a gentle golden glow spilled across the corridor.

"This is... nicer than I expected," Derk murmured.

Tapestries clung to the walls, each one telling a different story. At first, they showed scenes of serene forests, noble knights, and battles with dragons and gnomes. Further along, the imagery shifted: the building of castles, the rise of Scarllend, and the start of the civil war. It was a woven chronicle of the nation's soul. A strange warmth emanated from the tapestries, almost as if they held magic.

Billy was mesmerized, seeing the history of their land flashing before him in vivid detail. Ryker and Derk, though more seasoned, were amazed as well. Ryker studied creatures he did not recognize and wondered if these were the beings the king had sent him to find.

The trio walked for hours until exhaustion set in. They stopped to rest. Ryker propped their torches against the stone wall and unpacked food—buns, fruit, and plenty of jerky.

He was the first to fall asleep, weary from the emotional toll of battle and farewells. Derk and Billy stayed up longer. In typical fashion, Derk tried to scare Billy with cave monster tales.

"These caves were made by monsters," he whispered, wide-eyed. "Bet they're watching us right now."

Billy laughed nervously, but the stories stuck with him. Later, as he drifted off, he dreamed of creatures clinging to the ceiling—orange-striped skin, a single glowing green eye. They crawled silently toward him. He screamed—and woke with a jolt. Ryker and Derk were sitting by a crackling fire, sipping coffee.

"Bad dream?" Ryker asked.

"Yeah... I guess."

"Well, no more sleeping in," Derk said with a chuckle. "Eat up. We're moving soon."

They saddled up and pressed on. The murals continued along the walls, evolving with every step. Billy examined the images closely, absorbing Scarllend's turbulent past.

They travelled through the tunnels for two more days, stopping at night to rest and feed the horses—and themselves. The entire journey, the walls shifted with new scenes of history. They often wondered how the passage remained so pristine and who had placed the tapestries there in the first place.

It was a mysterious path.

They suspected the Burrowers had something to do with it, according to the legends they had heard. Yet they found it odd they had not seen a single one. Ryker remembered a story Shorpal had once told—that the Burrowers helped destroy the Volcanic Empire over 800 years ago. Yet, there were no depictions of them in the murals, even in the scenes of the collapsing mountain.

The Burrowers were said to be peaceful but private. They did not like to be disturbed. No one in the castle had seen them, except for Shorpal and the king. Neither spoke openly about their existence, only their history. Ryker had also heard they were nearly impossible to reason with. Only those with strong powers could communicate with them telepathically, though the Burrowers could read every thought or intention of those around them.

No one saw them—except Billy.

Each night, the young squire swore he saw the two-limbed protectors of the mountain.

Eventually, the smooth corridor gave way to jagged rock. Three paths branched off, each much darker than the main stretch they had crossed. Exhausted, they stopped to rest once more. Just above them, on the tapestry, they saw something new —three travellers, watched from above by strange, two-armed creatures.

"Burrowers," Ryker muttered. "They're here."

He had heard they were peaceful, but no one truly knew. A sense of caution crept into his bones. They set up watches for the night. Ryker took the first shift, then woke Derk, who in turn woke Billy.

Billy, alert and eager, leaned against the wall with his blade ready—until a rock fell from the ceiling, knocking him unconscious.

They awoke to find a newly dug path before them. What had been a blank wall the night before was now a dark tunnel. Ryker looked up at the tapestry above. The images now depicted their journey, their night of rest, and the Burrowers hovering nearby.

His blood ran cold.

"Time to move," he barked. "Now."

They packed in silence. None of them wanted to know what image might appear next.

The tunnel stretched onward. Though they saw no more signs of the Burrowers, they began to believe the creatures had cleared the path for them—perhaps to help them on their journey. Still, it remained dark. Time passed without sun or stars to guide them. The new section of the tunnel had no murals, as if the Burrowers had carved it hastily, just enough to allow them and the horses to pass through.

They were weary but pressed forward until a massive stone door blocked their path. Ryker stepped up, placed a palm against the center, and the stone slid away in four pieces. It had the same lock mechanism as the castle.

Sunlight blinded them. They emerged onto a rocky cliff, the afternoon sun hanging high. Below, a forest stretched endlessly, with smoke curling from what appeared to be a nearby village.

Ryker pointed. "Let's stop in that town—get some coffee, food, rest."

They slid down the rocky hill. Ryker led the way, his horse skidding expertly. Billy followed, eyes wide. Derk was last. His horse slipped, sending him sprawling. The squire burst out laughing, and Ryker quickly joined in.

"Not funny," Derk muttered as Ryker and Billy laughed.

"Then why are we laughing?" Ryker teased.

"Because you're an idiot," Derk replied, red-faced.

Dusting himself off, he rejoined the others on the trail. Soon, they spotted two ogres lounging between tall rocks. Ryker held up a hand, signaling for silence. They dismounted and hid their horses in the underbrush.

Ryker crept close enough to overhear.

"The ogre king's sending troops into Scarllend," one said.

"So? That ain't our problem," the other grunted.

"You better pick a side. Lord Diablo and Big Gor won't be kind to ogres who stay neutral. We swamp ogres don't stand a chance against the mountain army."

"Ah, banix," the first ogre growled, smashing the rock he was leaning on.

The impact shifted a loose stone that crashed down—nearly crushing Ryker and the others. The ogres spotted them.

"Spies! Knights!" they roared.

The trio sprinted for their horses. A boulder flew, smashing a tree beside them. Another blocked their exit. With no choice, they turned and drew their blades.

The ogres charged. Derk dodged an attack, and one of the creatures fell flat on its face. Billy rode wide, trying to circle around. Ryker charged straight through, slicing one ogre's hand off, then slashing its shin. It howled and collapsed.

"I'll get you, you sons of—" the ogre bellowed.

"Not today, arsehole!" Billy yelled as they galloped away.

Smoke from the nearby town rose ahead. A sign greeted them:

Town of Bowerville – A Locally Guarded Community

Centaurs patrolled the streets. They flanked the newcomers silently. Ryker, Derk, and Billy kept their heads down. The presence of the centaurs made them uneasy. Ryker had never dealt with the creatures before, but everyone knew they could be dangerous if provoked.

That, perhaps, was why they were there.

As they entered the main square, townspeople began to appear. The tavern stood near the edge of the forest—their destination. Out of nowhere, the centaurs reappeared. One smacked Billy's back, nearly knocking him off his horse.

"Go about your business," the centaur said flatly.

Then they turned and vanished.

Ryker exhaled. The centaurs, protectors of the forest, had an alliance with Bowerville. The trio had entered a neutral zone—for now.

The town bustled quietly. Villagers eyed the newcomers with curiosity as they dismounted. The scent of stew and baked bread drifted from the tavern's open windows—a welcome invitation after their long trek.

Ryker looked to the others. "Let's get something warm in our bellies. We'll need to rest before heading toward Crandrop tomorrow."

Billy rubbed the back of his head where the rock had struck him. "As long as I don't see any more monsters tonight, I'll sleep like a rock."

Derk chuckled. "After the caves, even a straw bed sounds like a royal throne."

Together, they headed into the tavern, unaware of what the night—or the next leg of their journey—might bring.

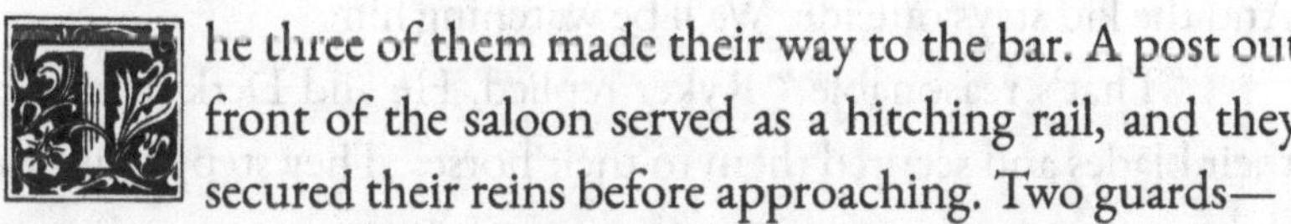

he three of them made their way to the bar. A post out front of the saloon served as a hitching rail, and they secured their reins before approaching. Two guards—both human—stood on either side of the tavern door, clubs in hand and machete-like blades at their hips. Fierce and stern-faced, they bore tattoos and the hardened look of old soldiers.

Ryker and Derk moved forward with Squire Billy following closely behind.

One guard stepped out and barked, "Tell that boy not to move any closer." He shook his club. "He's way too damn young to be in here."

The second guard blocked the door. "What are two knights of Scarllend and some kid doing here? Didn't you get the memo? We take care of ourselves now. We could've used your army years ago—back when the ogres tried taking over and the orcs got near. The centaurs and other foresters helped, along with the townsfolk. Now the enemy doesn't bother us, so we don't bother with them. No thanks to your army. Now what's your business in our tavern?"

Billy froze, his chest tight. Ryker and Derk stood their ground.

"You've got a pretty big mouth," Derk muttered.

"Huh?" growled the first guard.

Ryker stepped in calmly. "My apologies. I am Commander Ryker of the Scarllend Royal Forces. We are on official business and simply stopping for a quick meal before heading across the Majestic Forest. Three coffees, three meals, and then we'll be gone."

The guards exchanged glances, rubbing their chins. One finally nodded. "If the centaurs let you this far, you must not be too dangerous. You can enter—but leave your weapons out here. And the kid stays outside. We'll be watching him."

"That's reasonable," Ryker replied. He and Derk detached their blades and secured them to their horses. They stepped inside the tavern.

The saloon was smoky and dim, filled with rough-looking patrons. Old country music played from a bullfrog perched on a stool—it was not singing, but the sound flowed from its wide-open mouth like a living jukebox.

Two wild-looking men with thick blond beards and plaid jackets sat in the back corner—unmistakably lumberjacks. Even in this crowd, they stood out.

Ryker and Derk found seats at the bar. The bartender, a green-skinned, one-eyed lizard-like being with a long tail and an apron, greeted them. "What can I get you boys?"

"Three coffees and three orders of ribs and chicken legs," Ryker said.

"Make mine a draft instead of coffee," Derk added, earning a look from Ryker. But he said nothing.

Ryker paid with silver coins from a small purple pouch. The bartender vanished into the kitchen, then returned with drinks.

Just as they settled in, a slender man swaggered over. "What the hell are two knights doing in our town? Didn't you get the message—we don't want you here."

"We're just passing through," Ryker answered calmly.

"We don't care. We've been fine without the army. You just show up now to collect taxes?"

"Come on now, Craig," the bartender warned.

"They're nosing around where they don't belong."

A young lumberjack shouted from the back, "Yah, shut up, Craig! They'd kick your ass."

"I'll shut up, all right," Craig muttered. He turned to walk away—then spun and hurled his beer, splashing both knights. Ryker grimaced. Derk rose with fury in his eyes, towering over him. The room grew tense.

Craig laughed and turned as if to walk away—but then sucker-punched Derk, drawing blood. Derk did not hesitate. He picked Craig up and threw him across the room, smashing a table. The bar erupted.

A dozen angry patrons surrounded them, forming a semi-circle. One charged at Ryker with a blade. Ryker grabbed his wrist, snapped it, and flipped him to the floor.

The fight was on.

Ryker and Derk, weaponless, fought with fists and grit. Ryker dropped opponents with precise punches. Derk used brute strength and takedowns. But soon, they were outnumbered. Six large men pinned them, choking and pummeling.

Then—two chairs crashed down on their attackers.

The blond lumberjacks had joined the fight. Ryker and Derk broke free. Ryker slammed a man's head into the bar. Derk dodged punches and turned the tide.

The younger lumberjack kneed one of the attackers, then delivered uppercuts until the man dropped. The older one hurled another into the bar, knocking two more down. The bartender kept polishing glasses, unbothered.

Only one attacker remained. Ryker traded brutal punches with him until the younger lumberjack smashed a mug over the man's head. Dazed, he staggered. Ryker finished him with a slam to the bar.

All four turned on the final foe and brought him to the ground. Just as they neared the door, the tavern guards reappeared, axes raised.

The older lumberjack hurled a table at them. The guards chopped it mid-air and charged. One fought Ryker in a grapple for the axe. The others danced around wild swings. They were at a standstill—until Billy charged in.

He leapt onto the back of Ryker's opponent. Ryker disarmed the guard and struck him twice with the flat of the blade. The man collapsed.

The five now outnumbered the final guard. Billy swept his legs, and they brought him down.

"Let's get the hell out of here!" shouted the younger lumberjack.

They bolted to their horses. As centaurs rounded the corner, the two lumberjacks mounted up and led the way.
"Follow us!" they yelled.

Ryker rallied everyone and took the front. They galloped directly toward the forest. As they dashed through town, they kicked up dust with the centaurs in hostile pursuit. The group rode tightly together, the lumberjacks in the lead, the knights close behind, and their loyal squire following fast.

Derk and Ryker were immensely proud of Billy. He had already proven himself a tremendous help. Many thoughts crossed Ryker's mind. He now knew he was on a true adventure, doing exactly what the king had asked—uniting with anyone willing to help. He may have even met two more allies. He felt, for the first time, the weight of leadership. And he knew he was up to the challenge, even if he was venturing into unfamiliar forest lands with complete strangers.

The centaurs chased after them, shouting threats. One yelled, "You come back and we'll kill you, you bloody scoundrels!"

Just before they turned off the trail into the woods, the young lumberjack at the front shouted, "Not today, you big horse's ass!"

They escaped into the dense woods. The lumberjacks moved swiftly, weaving through thick trees and brush. Eventually, they reached a small clearing.

A rustic A-frame cabin stood there, its windows barred and curtained. A cast-iron pot simmered over a firepit. A small stable housed two horses, while the others were tied to nearby trees. Mesh hung around the stable to keep insects out.

"Well, it's good to see knights in these parts again," said the older lumberjack. "I'm Don. That's my son, Jason. You boys must be hungry."

They exchanged handshakes. Don led them inside the cabin. A fireplace sat at the back, with stairs overhead. A large Scarllend shield hung between them. Armor lined the walls. A sturdy oak table dominated the room.

Don served steaming bowls of beans from the wood stove.

"You must be on a mission. Ryker, was it? I noticed you never got your meal back at the tavern."

Ryker nodded. "Yes, I am Commander Ryker. We are headed to Crandrop to recruit support for the kingdom."

Don leaned back. "That's a tough town. What happened to Shorpal?"

"He died in battle."

Don lowered his head. "Every man's time comes. He was a good one."

"And you, sir?" Ryker asked. "You clearly served. I do not recall seeing you in the castle."

"Long story," Don said. "I grew up near Shantrock. Joined the Scarllend army at ten years old. I only trained at the castle for a few years before heading home to battle. We fought the orcs for years. When the kingdom stopped sending help, Shorpal went back to the castle. I stayed. Eventually, I settled here and forgot all about those days."

Ryker was impressed. "Well, you must be older than you look. We overheard ogres talking about joining Shantrock and the orcs."

Don's face darkened. "Well, that changes things. We need to warn the forest allies."

They finished their meal quickly. Jason poured more coffee. Don offered a calming pipe to ease their aches. As night fell, they agreed it was time to move. Don grabbed his gear, lit a sweet-smelling cigar, and led them out.

Lanterns were lit and tied to the horses. They rode into the darkening woods, guided only by flickering light—and the growing weight of the journey ahead.

As they walked out of the cabin, Ryker found himself overwhelmed by visions of his wife, the sweet and beautiful Petunia back home. She danced through his mind, lifting his spirit. Her image gave him hope and energy to journey on through the night.

CHAPTER 5

fter a winding, dark journey through the forest filled with twisting paths and thick brush, the group reached a hilltop. Don raised a hand and whispered,

"We will set up camp here for the night. It is far too late to disturb them."

Ryker and his companions peered through the trees. Here and there, soft flickers of golden light reflected off the branches. They spread out their sleeping bags under the open sky—the weather was mild, and no shelter was needed. Don and Jason set up hammocks between the trees and settled in for the night.

Exhaustion took hold quickly—until Ryker jolted awake with a sharp scream. He struggled, barely able to move, wrapped tightly in a thick net. His cry startled the others, but before they could react, they too were caught and bound. Don and Jason were tangled inside their hammocks, now twisted tight like cocoons.

They were being dragged—by small figures wearing pointed hats, each no taller than sixteen inches. Though diminutive, the gnomes moved with astonishing strength and precision. It took four to carry one human, but their teamwork was flawless. As the men squirmed, the nets tightened, making escape impossible.

Billy fumbled for his knife, but it slipped from his grip and fell through the net. One of the gnomes caught it mid-air and let out a gleeful laugh.

The forest gave way to a glimmering clearing. Golden lights glowed all around. Above them, rope bridges connected towering trees. Below, hundreds—perhaps thousands—of mushrooms sprouted in vibrant hues, each one seemingly alive with energy. In the center, a wide path led to a colossal tree stump crowned with a magnificent mushroom.

They were dropped in front of the stump. A small door and a single round window were carved into its base. It resembled a house—no, a palace. The mushroom on top mirrored the symbol of Scarllend.

Dozens of gnomes surrounded them. Some were squat and round, others lean and unusually tall for their kind. The door opened. A shadow appeared first, followed by an elderly gnome with wrinkled skin, crooked buck teeth, and a golden, jewel-encrusted hat. He wore a flowing velvet robe trimmed with gold and held a scepter topped with a glittering golden mushroom.

He stepped forward, frowning. "What in the blazes is going on out here?" he barked. Then, catching sight of the captives, he added, "What have you brought me now?"

Don grunted from his hammock. "Ronco! It's us—Don and Jason. We brought allies!"

Ronco raised a bushy eyebrow. "Well, you could've come earlier.
It's too late for guests, but since I'm up... bring them in!" He waved his scepter. "Release them, boys."

The gnomes cut the nets, and the humans tumbled free. With a flick of Ronco's scepter, they all shrank—each no taller than a gnome. Once they were at his level, Ronco led them into the giant stump.

Inside was a grand hall—at least from their shrunken perspective. The ceilings soared above them. A spiral staircase wound upward, and the space resembled a cross between a palace and a cottage. A golden square table stood in the center, adorned with silver mushroom carvings. At its head sat a silver-and-gold throne with the symbol of Scarllend gleaming at the top.

Ronco sat down and poured tea from a steaming pot.
"I figured you boys would show up eventually. Heard you made a mess in Burrowville. Thought you'd come crawling here looking for help, like always." He laughed.

Don chuckled. "You know us too well. These are Squire Billy, Sir Derk, and Commander Ryker—the new leader of the Scarllend army."

Ronco stared at Ryker. "Well, I'll be. A fresh commander, eh? So Shorpal's finally gone?"

Ryker nodded solemnly. "He died in battle."

Ronco sighed. "He was getting too old for that job, but it's a loss. Welcome, Ryker. Now tell me—what brings you here?"

"We're headed to Crandrop to recruit their private army and any other allies we can. We also wanted to alert you that ogres are planning an attack. We ran into some on the way and overheard them making plans."

"Crandrop, huh? Keith and his lot. Not a bad choice. Can't say they'll join, though. Still—it's something." Ronco puffed his pipe, blowing purple smoke into the air. "We've been guarding this forest, keeping ogres to the south. They're too stupid to make real plans—too stupid to even make it out of the swamps. With the help of the centaurs, they'll never get anywhere. The centaurs keep good protection over these parts. And after your little stunt in Burrowville, I doubt they'll be quick to help you."

Ryker winced. "We're aware. But we need every ally we can find. I've heard of many tribes in these parts. I imagine you know them."

Ronco nodded. "I'll speak to the elves. Lord Siamac still holds sway in the forest. He's much older than I am. Siamac was leader of the high elves in a distant land. He came to the Majestic Forest over a thousand years ago to watch over the wood elves and keep peace in the region. Long before my time. I'll send messengers to our cousins, the dwarves too. But it will be a long time before we hear anything. Their home lies in the northeast mountains, past the Scarllend border—even past Shantrock. There's a nation. Then he turned to his longtime friends. "You two take your chances with the pixies. May the stars be with you."

The map felt strange in Ryker's hand—ancient, weathered, and faintly humming with energy. The parchment looked as if it could crumble at any moment, yet it held firm, as if magically protected. When he concentrated, he noticed a faint glow radiating across its surface.

Then, as if in answer to his thoughts, the word Crandrop shimmered into view. A soft red line stretched across the map, marking a path only he could see.

It sent chills through his fingers and along his spine. There was something deeply mystical about the object—something alive.

CHAPTER 6

hey made their way back through the mushroom village, following the same path that had led them into the forest's strange heart. Their horses were still tied up where they had camped the night before. Before parting, King Ronco handed Ryker the fragile, ancient-looking map to Crandrop, along with a leather bag full of provisions.

As Ryker gripped the map, he felt a beam of confidence and warmth pass through his body. Though it looked like it might crumble into dust, it felt strong and durable in his hands.

Inside the bag were several types of mushrooms, small glass jars filled with coloured dust, and a few tightly sealed vials.

"The red ones are for regrowth," Ronco had explained vaguely, "and some of the others are... well, magic. You'll figure it out."

Ryker examined the contents with a mix of curiosity and confusion.

The mushrooms looked harmless enough, but the jars shimmered with a soft glow, and the dust inside seemed to shift colour when the light caught it. Before Ryker could ask for more details, Ronco chuckled, tapped his golden sceptre against the ground, and vanished in a puff of smoke—reappearing high above them on the rope bridge canopy, already alerting the village watch.

The gnomes had once led a great forest army. It had been more than a decade since they last mobilized—back when they pushed out the final leprechaun clans. Those battles, Ryker recalled from tales, were vicious. The leprechauns had once been known for stealth, illusions, and deadly trickery, but centuries of war had left them scattered and presumed extinct. Ronco had mentioned their last stand came after false promises from Lord Diablo—a painful echo of what Ryker now feared for the rest of Scarllend.

The leprechauns and gnomes had been at war even before Ronco was born. The leprechauns had once lived in the Majestic Forest until they overstayed their welcome. They constantly tried to outdo the magic of the gnomes. For reasons long forgotten, the two groups hated each other. The leprechauns attempted to invade the gnome village several times until the other forest tribes finally expelled them.

After being exiled, they settled in Shantrock for centuries. When Diablo rose to power, he struck a deal with them to invade the forest, promising military support. But the leprechauns were out-tricked. Once the majority had left their home, Diablo wiped out those who remained. The rest were believed to have died in battle. No one had heard anything of them in over a decade.

Once they left the mushroom village, Ryker mounted his

horse, the others following suit. Don and Jason veered east, heading toward the hidden Pixie Kingdom, while Ryker turned north, bound for the fortified town of Crandrop.

"Before you go," Ryker asked, holding up the bag, "can either of you tell me what this stuff actually does?"

Don laughed and nudged Jason. "He's better at remembering these things than I am."

Jason walked over and dug through the bag. He held up a tiny jar of golden dust. "This is pixie dust—good for healing and exhaustion. Brings a bit of euphoria too, so don't overdo it." He pulled out a couple of mushrooms next. "Red ones restore your normal size after shrinkage. The rest? Could do anything. Ronco says it's pure magic—but he wasn't exactly clear on how to use them."

Ryker nodded, pretending to feel more reassured than he actually was.

"Well, we're off to meet the Pixie Queen," Don said. "Hopefully she's in a forgiving mood. And Ryker—when you reach Crandrop, do not bring them back here. The map will show you the next meeting point when the time is right. Now, as you said: may the stars be with you."

Don gave him a firm handshake. Jason followed suit, clapping Ryker on the back with a grin. Then, with a final nod, they mounted their horses and disappeared into the dense eastern woods.

Ryker tucked the map inside his chest plate and led his companions deeper into the forest. The underbrush thickened quickly, and though he had only glanced at the map once, something inside him guided their way. It was as though the trail had been carved into his mind.

The path narrowed. The trees pressed tighter together. Just as Ryker began to doubt his direction, the woods opened up. A narrow trail stretched out before them—quiet, serene, and dappled in soft sunlight that pierced through the canopy above. The ground was packed dirt, scattered with golden leaves and ancient roots, leading north toward the unknown city of Crandrop.

ason and Don had a closer destination. They made their way on foot through the thick brush of the forest toward the place the pixies called home. It was a wide clearing with a large pond and a field of flowers blooming all around it. The pair arrived in the late afternoon, just after the pixies had finished their morning harvest from the abundant gardens.

They reached the valley with ease—this was not their first visit. Having lived in the forest for years, they knew the paths well. As they entered the area, they began to hear the fluttering of delicate wings and faint crackling sounds moving through the trees. Still, there was no sign of the pixies—until dust-like sparks began to flash and scatter toward them through the air.

They ducked, covering their mouths and noses with their shirts to avoid inhaling it. They managed to hold off the first wave, but suddenly the forest darkened. Sparks of green, red, blue, and yellow light burst around them like tiny fireworks.

Then, in front of them, a flash of white exploded like lightning, and they were hit head-on by the swirling lights.

Their vision blurred. Their minds spiraled. They could no longer see the forest. Instead, they were trapped in visions of nightmares—centaurs charging them, fire raining from the sky, shadowy warriors multiplying by the hundreds. Both men collapsed as their senses were overwhelmed by flame, darkness, and fear.

Then—nothing. Silence.

They awoke to a brilliant, golden glow. Their eyes fluttered open, struggling to adjust. All they could see were blurry, fluttering figures. A wand waved in front of their faces, and suddenly their vision cleared.

They realized they were now the size of pixies—tiny, tied up with vines against a rock, surrounded by several beautiful winged creatures.

Hovering just above them was the Pixie Queen herself. She was stunning, with long, pinned-up blond hair, a sleek black dress, and fiery emerald eyes that shimmered with charm or danger depending on her mood.

With a singsong voice, she said, "Well, well, well... long time no see. You must need something very important. Or could it be... you just missed us?"

Jason, still dazed, replied, "Well, of course we've missed helping you."

The Pixie Queen giggled. "Oh girls, did you hear that? They missed us!" The others laughed and gasped mockingly. "So what brings you here? Or are we just that irresistible?"

Jason cleared his throat. "There's something important going on. The leaders of the forest are being called for a meeting by the King's army.

The Queen's expression shifted. "The army? You mean the same army that once sent two sneaky traitors to steal the seeds of our secret flowers?" Her smile turned sinister. Her emerald eyes glowed red. As she grew angrier, the vines around Jason and Don tightened, and small thorns began to grow.

Then, with syrupy sweetness, she hovered in front of Jason, cupped his chin, and whispered, "What do you think those two traitors would say to me if they were here now?"

Jason, clearly under her spell, murmured, "I'm sure they were very sorry... maybe even tricked."

"That's nonsense!" Don shouted. "Wake up, boy! These pixies were trading their magic to manipulate the creatures of the forest —and Ronco stopped it with fair trade!"

The Queen snarled and grabbed Don by the throat. "What did you just say to me? Why did Ronco send you here?"

Don tried to resist, but under her influence, he muttered, "He feared you were becoming too powerful..."

The Queen suddenly released him and grinned. "So the old man feels threatened. I guess maybe he won't be able to resist me again—like when he was young and still had brains? How flattering." Then she leaned back and cooed, "You boys aren't afraid of me, though, are you?"

"No, Miss Tiffany," they both said in unison.

"Good. I wouldn't want to cast a spell just to calm your nerves," she teased, twirling her hair. "So... why should we help you in your little war?"

Don replied, "The new Chief wants to unite Scarllend. Shantrock is gaining too much ground. Without unity, we'll lose the forest—and the kingdom. We need all four sorcerers of the Majestic Forest."

"Who else are you recruiting?" she asked, crossing her arms.

Jason added, "Ronco is meeting with Lord Siamac, and our Chief is on his way to Crandrop."

The Queen raised an eyebrow. "Do you silly fools really think Keith and his men will help?"

Jason hesitated. "I don't know. But we've come this far. If we don't try, we'll never stand a chance against Shantrock."

Tiffany hummed and tapped her lip. "Hmm. The pixies can survive on their own. But I do hate smelly ogres." She narrowed her eyes. "You remember the leprechaun war, don't you?"

"We do," Don said. "And Diablo sent them—just like he's recruiting orcs and ogres now. It could be even worse."

The Queen nodded slowly. "Fine. I'll consider joining. But Ronco had better keep his old mouth shut."

"Yes, Miss Tiffany," they said again.

"Now then," she said, suddenly chipper, "when and where is this grand meeting?"

Jason and Don exchanged blank stares. They had no idea. Ronco never told them.

Jason scrambled. "Messenger birds! Ronco will send one when the time comes—it's all very... top secret."

Tiffany narrowed her eyes, unconvinced, then sighed. "That does sound like something he'd do. So... what should I do with you two traitors?"

Don said quickly, "Maybe let us go back to the gnome village and wait there?"

"Oh, no no no," she said, fluttering closer. "If you want my help, I'll be needing yours first." Her eyes gleamed as the vines loosened. "We have a very special task for you."

Both men gulped.

Moments later, pixies carried the two men—still shrunken—across the sparkling pond and vibrant flower fields, through the woods to a giant tree covered in thorny vines.

"Until the old coot sends his bird," Tiffany said, "you'll be picking pollen off those flowers. Any objections?"

"No, Miss Tiffany!" they replied in sync.

The pixies dropped small nets and tweezers into their hands. Tiffany smirked. "Don't have too much fun." Then, she vanished into the woods.

Jason and Don looked at each other—alone, but not unwatched.

Tiffany had left two of her top girls to guard them and keep them under enchantment. Both were stunning, seductive, and just as manipulative as their queen.

Dominus, one of the guards, had deep, chocolate-toned skin and long flowing black hair. Her commanding presence was unmatched. When she spoke, her tone was firm and serious, and she always meant business. Jason had long harboured a secret crush on her. She was a master of mental enchantment—and torture.

Thali, the second, had tanned skin, sharp hazel eyes, and luscious brown curls. Sassy and flirtatious like Tiffany, she could also switch to stern authority when needed, much like Dominus.

With their combined powers—and hypnotic beauty—Jason and Don stood no chance of escape.

CHAPTER 8

Ryker and his two companions travelled for hours on end. A few times, Ryker stopped to make sure his instincts matched the map—and every time, they did. The trail on the map aligned perfectly with his intuition, drawing them steadily toward the northern edge of the forest, where Crandrop awaited.

They spent the day moving on pure instinct, taking several winding turns through the dense path. Conversation was scarce. All three men focused on their surroundings—the sounds of birds, crickets, and the occasional rustling through the trees. Though nothing had approached them yet, each had the uneasy sense that they were being watched. The forest was home to countless creatures, and they had no idea which ones might be tracking them.

As the afternoon faded and the sky bled red through the treetops, Ryker's instincts flared. Before he even heard the sound, he felt the danger. He glanced back at Derk and Billy, then pointed into the woods. Without a word, they dashed into the underbrush. Shadows moved. Gruff voices echoed nearby.

Panicked but quick-thinking, Ryker grabbed the bag of mushrooms and dust given to him by Ronco. He pulled out a handful of mushrooms, held a finger to his lips to signal silence, then pointed at the horses. Each of them fed two mushrooms to themselves and their mounts—and immediately shrank down to gnome size.

Ryker did not know how he recalled that so quickly—it was pure instinct.

Two centaurs approached, bodies broad and armored, battle axes in hand, speaking amongst themselves.

"Did you just see that tree move?"

"Yes. I heard they were spotted around here. Maybe they're in the treeline."

The knights and squire sat low in their saddles, tiny and hidden in the foliage. Ryker guided them into a tight space beneath the brush. Even at their shrunken size, the overhanging branches brushed their heads. They were swallowed by a dark tangle of vines and leaves.

"I don't see anything," one centaur said.

The other started swinging his axe into the bushes. Branches fell all around the hidden trio.

Ryker hesitated—then did the unthinkable. He led them toward the centaurs, skirting the edge of the newly opened clearing. They galloped right beneath the hooves of the two beasts, darted through more brush, and emerged into another narrow path—just in time.

The centaurs looked down, confused, but the trio was already gone.

"I guess it was just a critter," one muttered.

"Yeah. Let's keep heading that direction."

The danger passed, but Ryker knew it was not gone for good.

They continued deeper into the forest, Ryker relying on his inner compass. By nightfall, they found a small clearing off the trail. He gave another round of mushrooms to the men and horses, returning them all to full size. They made camp quickly—no fire, just exhaustion and caution.

Ryker's bag began to glow. He opened it to find several mushrooms shining softly, like magical flashlights. He placed them around the site, casting a soft, safe light. The men rolled out their sleeping bags and tried to rest. They were starving and low on supplies, wishing they had something more than mystical mushrooms.

As they lay there, a distant howling echoed. At first, it sounded peaceful. Billy and Derk drifted off quickly. Ryker did not. His gut warned him something was coming. The howls grew louder. The branches swayed. The horses grew restless, stamping and snorting.

Ryker stood, sword in hand, glowing mushroom in the other. As he peered into the brush near the horses, he saw two red eyes staring back.

A werewolf leapt out, landing on Ryker with terrifying force. He blocked it with his shield as it snapped and slashed. One of the horses kicked the beast, but it turned and clawed the animal down with a shriek.

Before it could kill the other two horses, a single arrow pierced its throat. Billy stood nearby, bow in hand, breathing heavily.

Another werewolf lunged. Derk helped Ryker to his feet and slashed it down in the same movement.

Ryker yelled, "We need to go—now!"

"But where?" Derk asked.

"We'll find our way. Pack what you can. You two ride together. Follow me."

Derk, bleeding and panicked, snapped, "Why should we follow you? Billy just saved your ass. We should've stayed at the castle!"

Ryker gritted his teeth. "Then if I fail, I'll resign. But right now, we have to move!"

Suddenly—a slash.

Derk screamed. Another werewolf tore into him, slicing deep into his side.

Billy fought back, stabbing the beast in the gut. Ryker beheaded it with a single blow—then turned and spun to strike down another.

Derk writhed on the ground, bones visible through torn flesh. Ryker rifled through the mushroom bag, panicked. He grabbed a glowing mushroom and the golden pixie dust.

"Eat it," Ryker ordered.

"Why should I trust you?"

"Because you'll die if you don't!"

Derk bit the mushroom. Ryker sprinkled the dust on his wounds.

The change was instant. The wounds closed. The pain faded. Derk's body surged with energy, his vision glowing gold.

Another beast appeared. Derk sprang up, dagger in hand, and drove it through the creature's throat. His movements were fluid —almost superhuman.

He turned to Ryker and shouted, "Let's go!"

They mounted quickly. Billy jumped on with Derk. Ryker secured glowing mushrooms to their horses for light and led the way.

The howls faded, but the danger remained. They weaved through brush, red eyes still watching.

Ryker's instincts took over. The trail revealed itself. They followed it north.

Eventually, the eyes disappeared. The howls grew distant. Ryker told Derk to slow down. Both men agreed: they had escaped—for now. But they could not stop.

They rode on through the night—searching for the next safe place to rest.

CHAPTER 9

he night had been long for everyone. Ryker and his troops travelled through the dark forest with nothing but instinct to guide them, exhausted and sleep-deprived. Jason and Don were still trapped under the pixies' control, while even Ronco, king of the gnomes, had not managed a wink of rest.

Ronco had flown a great distance to reach the elves' kingdom. There were smaller colonies scattered throughout the region, but most of the elves lived deep in the forest under the guidance of their leader, Lord Siamac.

The elven kingdom was modest but enchanting. There were no towering castles like those in Scarllend or Shantrock—just elegant wooden huts built around a stony creek that meandered through the trees. At the top of the village stood a wide, cascading waterfall. Perched on the cliff beside it was a large barn-style hall, used for festivals and council gatherings.

Above the falls, nestled near a tranquil pond dotted with lily pads, stood a small tower. A stream fed into the pond, its waters glinting under moonlight. Ronco flew toward the tower, shrinking himself and entering through an open window. With a puff of light, he grew to full size and landed beside a table still much bigger than him.

An old elf let out a startled gasp. The elf—long white beard, deeply lined skin, and pointed ears sticking out from under a striped nightcap—was reclining in pale blue-and-white pajamas, puffing from an emerald hookah. Then he shook his head.

"I knew you were coming, my old friend," he said, exhaling a swirl of red smoke from his nose.

Ronco chuckled. "You say you were expecting me, and yet you nearly jumped out of your skin."

"I wasn't expecting you at this hour. You, of all people, know it's not proper to intrude on someone while they're sleeping."

"I'm very sorry, Sam. But if you thought I was asleep, why are you still awake?" Ronco asked.

"I haven't been able to sleep. I could feel something stirring. Besides, I've been keeping an eye on the forest—and your friends."

"Yeah, the centaurs didn't exactly roll out the welcome mat."

"No, they're a grumpy bunch," the elf agreed. "You're lucky I'm a little friendlier. Who were the men travelling with them? They looked like knights. Something we haven't seen around here in a long time."

"They're not just any knights. One of them is the new chief of Scarllend's military."

The elf, Lord Siamac, leaned forward. "So the rumours were true—Shorpal has fallen."

Ronco nodded solemnly.

"And now they're trying to unite the country again," Siamac added. "You've come to recruit us, haven't you?"

"You know me too well," Ronco replied. "The darkness is growing again. It's getting stronger, and closer."

Siamac sighed and gestured to a wooden stool. "Sit. Rest. You look like hell—but then again, you always do."

Ronco smirked and sat down. "You're lucky that mouth of yours hasn't gotten you killed."

"Ah, my friend, in the thousands of years I've lived, it hasn't yet. I must be doing something right."

Ronco pulled out his pipe, and the two shared smoke in silence before diving into conversation. They spoke for over an hour, recounting recent events, reminiscing about old spells, and strategizing like they had so many times before.

They also spoke of the darkness they had both felt. When Daniel Sable discovered Scarllend, the Volcanic Empire—buried deep in the mountains atop Shantrock—was the greatest threat to the free lands. A dark and fiery lord by the name of Blitzker commanded a grave and gruesome army and had managed to bring them to the surface.

Only with the help of every force in the region with any good in them were they able to strike down Blitzker's legions and drive them back to the fires of Volcanica—led by Daniel Sable himself. That was why he remained such an important figure in the land's history.

The Burrowers of the castle tunnels had helped collapse the mountain, sealing the enemy inside. As thanks, they were given the royal mountains as their home.

Ronco and Siamac had always feared the rise would happen again, and with each passing day, that feeling grew stronger.

"So," Siamac finally said, "tell me about these three men stirring up trouble. What's their plan in Crandrop?"

"They're hoping to recruit the warriors there. I don't know exactly what their plan is, but I believe in them. Jason and Don met them at the tavern and brought them to me."

"And where are they now?"

"They split up. Ryker took the map I gave him and headed for Crandrop. Jason and Don went to the pixies."

Siamac sat up straighter. "You gave your map to a stranger?!"

"He's the new chief. If anyone's trustworthy, it's him."

"You hope. And sending Jason and Don to the pixies? With your history? You know Tiffany has never forgiven you for breaking her heart two hundred years ago. Since you three are so close, she doesn't like them much either."

"I was planning to send a messenger bird once we had a meeting place. I just didn't expect everything to move this fast."

Siamac stood, now fully awake. "They could be in serious trouble. We need to send word. Tell Jason and Don to meet us at the base of the great waterfall in the heart of the forest once the knights arrive. I'll send a message to Crandrop and communicate with Keith."

He paused, looking Ronco over. "You should rest—but this might not wait."

"You're right," Ronco said, rising. "Time to see what kind of mess those witches have brewed up."

With a flash of light, Ronco shrunk himself. He stepped onto the windowsill, gave a sharp whistle, and a golden hawk came swooping down from the sky. He leapt onto its back and gave a final wave to Siamac.

"See you later, Sammy!"

Then he soared off into the trees, headed toward the pixie glen—where Jason and Don were still toiling under a charm spell, forced to work the thorn bushes through the night.

CHAPTER 10

hile Ronco made his way to see the pixies, Ryker, Derk, and their squire continued their journey to Crandrop. They had travelled through the night into the early morning, well before the rise of day. After hours of pushing forward along the same narrow trail, the sky began to shift into a soft purple haze—daybreak approaching at last.

Ryker could feel they were drawing near. The presence of the werewolves had faded; no sounds or signs remained. He decided this was the perfect moment to rest. A clearing peeked through the branches, just wide enough to camp. They unrolled their mats and hitched the horses. Ryker slept with the map clutched tightly to his chest. Though the gnome had said little about it, he trusted it held more power than it seemed—and that it needed to be protected.

All three of them fell into a deep, much-needed sleep.

But it was not sunlight that woke Ryker.

His eyes snapped open to cold steel pressing against his throat.

Out of the corners of his vision, he saw men closing in. Derk and Billy were already being tackled and bound with rope. They were under attack.

Ryker gripped the man's wrist, trying to twist the knife away, but two more attackers grabbed him from behind. He struggled to flip one of them over his shoulder, but they were too strong—even for the commander-in-chief of Scarllend. They slammed his back against a tree and began tying him tightly. Within minutes, all three soldiers were restrained. They had been completely overpowered.

The man who had held the knife to Ryker's throat now stood in front of him. He had wild, curly red hair and a thick beard to match—his eyes blazing with contempt. He lowered the blade to Ryker's chest, keeping it close.

"You knights are a little far from your guarded walls, aren't you?" the man sneered. "You should head back where it's safe. Looks like you lot can't handle yourselves out here—we just proved it."

"Listen," Ryker said firmly. "I am the new commander of the Scarllend army. My first mission is to recruit the knights of Crandrop. If I had to guess... you must be them?"

The man let out a harsh laugh, then punched Ryker hard in the stomach. He spat a thick stream of black juice onto Ryker's chest.

"Some chief you are," he snarled. "You don't even know your country's history. You're worse than Shorpal."

Ryker opened his mouth to respond, but the man raised the knife again.

"There's a reason people don't talk about us," he continued. "The king and his cronies would rather forget what they did."

Go on then," Ryker growled. "Tell me."

The red-haired man leaned in.

"We were a private platoon—Crandrop's own. We fought with your army until one day, word came that a massive force of orcs was headed our way. You know what your brave knights did? They left. In the middle of the night."

His voice dropped, colder now.

"They left us to die. We fought for days—thousands of orcs. I wasn't much older than that twerp over there," he gestured to Billy. "Now imagine what I saw. Imagine what I did."

He stepped back, fury cooling into bitterness.

"With the help of our leader, we rebuilt. We trained. We've survived. And we protect our own. You want us to help you now? After all that?" He paused, curling his lip. "I should kill you. Just to show the kid what war really looks like."

"We need to unite the country," Ryker said. "That's the only way we survive what's coming."

"No. You listen." The man sheathed his knife. "I'm not going to kill you—not yet. But I am taking you to the Keeper of our town. A real leader. One with great and powerful magic. I'm sure he's the one you came to see."

Without another word, the men hoisted the three soldiers—each bound hand and foot—and dragged them through the woods. They re-emerged on the main trail, where several more riders waited.

Each prisoner was strapped to a horse. Their own mounts were taken captive. Bags were tied over their heads, and they were knocked unconscious.

They were carried through the heart of Crandrop—a town of tight wooden houses clustered around a wide pond and a narrow creek. It was far more quaint than the castle they had come from, but much larger than Burrowville. Along the south side stood the Majestic Forest, and to the north rose the great mountains that marked the border of Scarllend.

Villagers watched silently, stepping aside to let the riders pass. The people looked strong and rugged. It was a town of warriors —men and women who lived in peace with one another.

The procession stopped outside a brutal-looking bar. It was an old brick building that looked like it had been falling apart for ages. The three men were taken inside and left to wait.

For what—or who—they did not yet know.

CHAPTER 11

s the morning approached, Ronco, the King of the Gnomes, neared the pixie gardens—ready to speak with Miss Tiffany face to face. When he arrived at the intoxicatingly aromatic and majestic grounds, the sun had just begun to rise, casting glistening light on the dew-covered petals and shimmering pond. The entire garden glowed in the golden wash of dawn.

Ronco flew low across the vibrant flower beds, but was suddenly stopped in his tracks. Miss Tiffany popped into view without warning, appearing directly in front of him. He halted mid-flight, nearly thrown from his bird companion.

She stood with her wand resting gently against her lips, one finger twirling a curl of hair, her eyes fixed on him with an unreadable smile.

"So, Ronco... you had the guts to come see me yourself," she said with a giggle. "Do not worry—your little thieves are fine.

I've been keeping them... safe. Now, what's so important that you left your mushroom town to actually do something?"

Ronco clenched his jaw, his expression turning sour.

"Listen—this is not a game. The forest needs your help. We always come together when the time calls for it, so enough with the foolishness."

"Foolish?" Tiffany raised an eyebrow, mock-offended. "You're the one who sent spies to steal from us—because you're scared your magic's going dull. Be honest, Ronco. This isn't about unity—it's about fear. You're just the king of mold, and we both know all your magic comes from it."

"Shut it." Ronco snapped. "All you do is manipulate the weak-minded. You've turned your 'trade agreements' into enslavement. That's not magic—it's control. Jason and Don aren't thieves—they were your pawns."

"Oh, Ronco," she sighed with delight, "those are just some of the perks of being a pixie."

"If you have any decency in your soul," he said, voice low and steady, "you'll use your power for something good. Shantrock is close to taking the castle. Once they do, they'll sweep across the land—and we'll all fall. Scarllend's last stronghold is the only thing keeping them from marching north."

Miss Tiffany fluttered in place, her smile sly. "I never said I wouldn't help," she said sweetly. "I just like watching you squirm. Making you mad is adorable. Now—what's the plan?"

"We'll rendezvous with Siamac and the Elves at High Falls. The new chief of the Scarllend military will meet us there."

"Then I guess it's time I show you where your 'friends' are," she grinned.

Tiffany fluttered ahead, and Ronco followed, flying just

above her. They passed the lush gardens and entered the rear grounds of pixie territory, where a dense wall of thorned roses tangled into an impassable thicket.

"Your nimrods are in there," she said. "Go fetch them." Ronco squinted at the thorns. He spotted Thali stationed within, watching over the area. It was clear Jason and Don were trapped—ensnared by magic and labour.

Ronco's eyes narrowed. Then, he did something guaranteed to infuriate her. He spiraled the hawk down directly toward the bush, then with a flick of his scepter, he blasted a shockwave of sparkling magic—blowing open part of the thorny wall.

Inside, Jason and Don were revealed—still shrunken and working furiously, The gorgeous pixie Dominus had been there all night using her powers to keep them working and following every single one of her commands. They looked like hell covered in sweat from head to toe.

Ronco swooped back to his bird and dove toward the pair. Ronco dove down flying right into the path he had cleared. Thali and Dominus launched forward to intercept, but Ronco fired a quick arc of energy from his scepter, stunning them and andsending her spiraling backward. The golden hawk lifted both Jason and Don, one in each claw—no trouble at all in their miniature state.

As Ronco soared into the sky, a horde of pixies rose to intercept him. Magic shards shot upward like darts, but Ronco summoned a golden dome of light from his scepter. It repelled the magic in all directions, knocking back most of the attackers. All but Tiffany.

She held steady, wings flapping fiercely as she raced toward him. Ronco turned back briefly and shouted over the winds:

"Do not forget! Meet us at High Falls. If you do not show, you're a traitor to the forest!"

Tiffany let out a shriek that echoed through the garden. She had been outmatched—and mocked. Though furious, she had made a promise in front of her people. And now, if she failed to honour it, Ronco would spread word of her treachery.

Worse—she knew he was right. Shantrock's threat was real. Tiffany narrowed her eyes. Old grudges or not, she would have to work with Ronco... once again.

CHAPTER 12

yker, Derk, and Billy woke abruptly with a pale of dirty water splashing them in a damp, dimly lit back room of a grimy tavern. Cold water dripped from their faces, their heads pounding as they slowly regained consciousness. The room smelled of mildew and rust—a janitor's room turned to makeshift holding cell, littered with dented pails, rotting mops, and a cracked stone sink. Along the far wall hung a row of aged weapons—swords, axes, and rusted bows. It looked like it was a small armory for those who worked at the bar.

Dozens of hard-faced soldiers loomed over them, weapons in hand, radiating hostility. Calahar—the wild-haired brute with the fiery beard the same man who had captured them—stood front and centre, A jagged knife in hand, his expression twisted with rage.

"So tell me," Calahar growled, stepping forward, "why I shouldn't kill you three right now?"

Before Ryker could answer, a voice from the shadows interrupted.

"That won't be necessary, Calahar."

From the darkness emerged an old man cloaked in black, his back hunched and gait deliberate. The tension in the room shifted. "Everyone out," the cloaked figure ordered. "I need to speak with them—alone."

The soldiers obeyed without hesitation.

"Except you, Calahar. You stay. Guard the door," the mysterious man added.

"Yes, sir," Calahar grumbled, stepping aside but keeping his axe close.

Once the room was cleared, the cloaked man turned to face the prisoners. Despite the shadows hiding most of his features, his presence commanded the room.

"You must be the two knights and the squire of the kingdom," he said. Then, with quiet precision, he pointed to each of them.

"You," he said to Billy, "must be the young squire." He looked to Derk. "Sir Derk." Then to Ryker. "And you—the new Commander-in-Chief of Scarllend, Mr. Ryker."

Ryker narrowed his eyes. "How do you know who we are? And if we were expected, why the warm welcome?"

The man chuckled dryly. "Word travels fast in these parts. I wanted your arrival kept quiet. The forest has ears, and not all who hear your names speak kindly."

He stepped closer, lowering his hood. His long silver hair fell over deep facial scars, and his eyes—pure white with no irises— seemed to look right through them. "My name is Keith. Leader of Crandrop's militia."

Calahar snorted. "They don't deserve to know who we are they are disgusting bastards," he shouted then spit black juice onto the floor.

"Calahar!" Keith barked. "I'm trying to have a conversation. And stop spitting on the damned floor."

Calahar sulked but obeyed.

Keith continued. "After your kingdom's army abandoned us during the Orc Wars, we were left to defend ourselves. Thousands of orcs descended on our towns. Many died. Calahar was barely older than your squire when it happened. That day changed us. Since then, we've built a true fighting force—trained, disciplined, independent. We were united with the Scarllend army untill a waive of orcs was sent by surprise. They devestated our town. The knights left saying they return with reinforcements but they never came and that is what made our people come together, and reject your kingdom."

Ryker listened in silence, absorbing the weight of history he hadn't lived through.

"I don't blame you personally," Keith said at last. "You weren't there. But many here still carry that wound. Calahar... was one of the boys left behind, and forced to fight for his life."

Keith turned to Calahar. " you may not agree but I say it is time we come together once more. Ready a small troop—volunteers only. We won't commit yet, but we'll prepare."

Calahar stepped forward, glaring. "You're really going to help these royal lapdogs?"

Keith's voice dropped low. "Siamac of the Elves and Ronco of the Gnomes have both called for unity. I won't ignore that—not after all we've lost. The old council is stirring again. Something's coming."

Calahar growled in disgust "well fine if it means that much to you but I don't trust them a lick," then he walked away slamming the door behind him.

Keith exhaled slowly. "You'll have to excuse him. Those who survived the Great Battle... they don't forget easily."

He looked back to Ryker, now with a measure of respect.

"Still, I believe this could be the beginning of peace. A second chance for Scarllend. I'll accompany you to the High Falls to meet Siamac and the others. As commander, it's only right you come. Derk, Billy—you'll remain here until Calahar deems it safe."

Before anyone could object, Keith stepped forward and placed a hand on Ryker's arm. A swirl of silver light encased them both, and in a flash, they vanished.

Derk and Billy sat stunned, still bound and dripping. The silence in the room felt like a storm waiting to break. All they could do now was wait—for a grudge-bearing warrior with a twitchy axe hand to decide their fate.

CHAPTER 13

yker awoke on his back in the middle of the forest, the sound of a rushing creek echoing nearby through a thick cluster of trees. He blinked up at the canopy overhead, dazed. His body was sore, his mind fogged, and his last memory was of being tied up in a dim back room—captured.

Suddenly, a strong grip yanked him upright. Keith, the old warrior of Crandrop, stood over him.

"A little puzzled, are we?" Keith smirked. Ryker's brow furrowed in confusion.

"For the chief of an army, you do not seem too familiar with your own land. Feels like you have never left the castle walls. Am I wrong?"

Ryker straightened, brushing off his shoulders. "Of course, I have left the castle. I have served my whole life." But even as he said it, doubt crept in. How much had he really known beyond the kingdom walls?

He thought about the vast forests, the old grudges, the magic of the gnomes and pixies—all of it foreign to him until now. Many times on this journey, he had thought these same things. But every event that had happened only made him want to strengthen himself and his army—to grow into a leader worthy of guiding his country, like Daniel Sable once did. He also wanted to ensure not only the safety of his land but his own as well, so that he could return home to his wife, whom he deeply missed, though he tried not to show it. His goal was to be as solid as a rock, though he was not quite there yet.

Keith chuckled. "Keep telling yourself that, kid. You might not know much about the world you are meant to protect, but you have the right demeanor. That is why I am bringing you with me—to speak with the elders of the forest."

Ryker frowned. "What do you mean by the right demeanor?" Keith shrugged, already moving ahead. "You will figure it out. Come on. We are already late."

They trekked through the woods, the trees slowly thinning, the creek widening beside them. The current grew stronger, and soon the faint roar of waterfalls echoed through the trees.

The forest opened to a majestic sight: a towering rock formation shaped like a jagged pyramid, carved by time and water. A massive waterfall cascaded down its center, feeding a crystal-clear pool at the base, which scattered into many streams that nourished the forest.

Keith stopped at the water's edge. Without warning, he grabbed Ryker's arm.

"What are you—" Ryker shouted.

"Do not fight it," Keith said, pulling them both into the roaring waterfall.

Ryker shut his eyes against the deluge. When he opened them, they were inside a stone chamber—a hidden cave behind the falls.

A large marble table sat in the center. Around it were familiar faces: Ronco, the old gnome king, perched on a tall chair just high enough to peek over the edge. Jason and Don stood in the corner, not yet welcomed to the table; the two were simply honoured to be there.

Three others Ryker did not know. An imposing centaur in black and red armor stood silently, his horns wide and battle-worn. His expression was unreadable—but clearly unimpressed. Sitting across the table was an old wizard with a long white beard —Lord Siamac, the elven leader, smoking from an emerald pipe.

Then, a voice sparkled like chimes. "Now that everyone's here, I suppose I will join."

Tiffany, queen of the pixies, fluttered into view, winking at Ryker. "Well, hello there, handsome," she cooed, then took her place at the table beside Ronco.

Keith pulled out a rough stone stool for Ryker and gestured for him to sit.

Siamac rose, pipe in hand. "I am very pleased to see everyone here once again, and I thank you all for coming. I know there are deep wounds and old grudges in this room. But dark times are ahead, and in these times, we must focus on what we share—this land. Scarllend is the land we have all protected for most of our lives. Like the great warriors before him, Ryker has journeyed far to be here and faced many barriers along the way."

The centaur, Butch, snorted loudly. "He's just another troublemaker!"

Siamac gave him a long look, then continued. "Shantrock's power grows. They take more land by the day.

The kingdom needs our power and soldiers, and Ryker is here seeking it. Commander Ryker—tell the forest what you have prepared."

Ryker hesitated. Siamac's piercing gaze made it clear he already sensed that Ryker did not have a formal plan.

Before he could speak, Butch growled, "Spit it out already, boy. We do not have all day. What kind of commander are you, anyway?"

Gasps echoed in the chamber. But something in Ryker shifted. He stood taller, voice firm.

"As chief of Scarllend's military, I was sent to recruit Crandrop's defenders. I have left behind my wife, my unborn child, my home. I have fought werewolves, survived ambushes, been beaten, and still I stand. I may not know everything—but I know this country cannot win if we fight alone."

"And you stirred up an entire town. I know what you fools did in Burrowville," Butch snapped.

"We were on a mission. I regret the chaos, but I will not apologize for fighting to protect our home."

Siamac nodded. "Let him finish."

Ryker continued, "My mission was to build a force strong enough to retake the castle gate—the last defense of Scarllend. If we lose it, the nation falls. But if we reclaim it, we can push east and take back our land—village by village—until we push Shantrock back to the mountains."

The chamber was quiet. Even Butch remained silent. Siamac turned to Tiffany. "Leader of the pixies, where do you stand?"

Tiffany twirled her hair. "I am glad you all thought of me, but I still do not like that old windbag."

"I did not want you here, you tricky pixie," Ronco barked. She grinned. "Well, if it means spending more time with these sweet boys..." she winked at Jason and Don, "...I suppose I am in. I would not want to see either of them hurt."

Siamac turned to Keith. "And where do you stand, my good friend?"

Keith nodded. "Ryker might be green, but he is brave. With Siamac, Ronco, and myself aligned, now is the time."

"With this decided," Siamac said, "Butch, great warrior and protector of the Majestic Forest, I ask you a favour of great responsibility."

Butch spoke in a commanding tone. "Lord Siamac, I am always ready to serve you, the forest, and the surrounding lands. I thank you for letting me stay here. I want nothing to do with this so-called commander—and especially nothing to do with those twits in the corner." He pointed to Jason and Don, who were just lucky enough to be invited.

"I thank you for your commitment to your home, which we have protected for ages," Siamac said. "You will need to prepare your own troops. There have been rumblings through the land of ogres planning an attack. With your great leadership, I trust you can handle anything they have in store."

"Understood, sir. I thank you again for your trust in me. My warriors and I have fought our hearts out keeping the ogres away. As a superior, I cannot stop you from leaving to protect this fool, so I will stand guard over the Majestic Forest."

Keith stood and turned to Ryker. "We shall gather our troops. May we all meet at the main pathway. Pack well. The journey to the castle will not be easy."

Keith placed a hand on Ryker's shoulder, and with a flash, they vanished.

Siamac rose. "May the rest of us do the same. Ronco, take the mortals back to the gnome village and prepare your fleet. Butch, I thank you for keeping your composure. And Miss Tiffany—do not forget that you are on our side."

Siamac shimmered into a ball of green light and disappeared. A final spell launched Butch forward—sending the centaur galloping through the falls.

Only Tiffany, Ronco, Jason, and Don remained.

"I do hope we can be friends," Tiffany purred. "I was quite awful before, was I not?"

Jason and Don approached her. "Apology accepted," Jason smiled.

Ronco raised his scepter. "That does not work on me, pixie." With a swirl of light, Ronco vanished with his companions—leaving Tiffany floating, fuming, and flustered in their wake. She thought about how much she hated Ronco because he had managed to see through her spells over two centuries ago. They had a complicated history. She had been much younger than Ronco when he became king and had used her charms to get whatever she wanted—including her own garden and pond. She had even tried to take full control of the gnome village until Ronco broke free of her influence and banished her to the pond she now ruled. She hated him for defeating her magic, and he hated her for taking what was once gnome territory.

eith and Ryker appeared just outside of Crandrop. This was Ryker's first time entering Crandrop while fully conscious. The village was filled with rows of log homes, quaint cabins, and barns. Farmlands spread across its outskirts, and a towering log wall encircled the entire area, its sharp points extending high into the air. Soldiers stood guard outside the main gate—two mounted on horseback and four stationed on foot, fully armed.

Keith led Ryker directly through the open gate without hesitation. As they entered, Ryker saw hundreds of men gathered throughout the streets—many seated atop horses, all clad in full armour with swords, bows, and axes at the ready. The town was alive with soldiers preparing for the coming war.

Deeper inside the village, a crowd had already formed. Calahar rode up to Keith and Ryker and said, "This is what we get when we arrive—they are already prepared."

"Quite impressive," Keith replied.

"You would be surprised how many here still want to unite the country."

Keith nodded. "I suppose not everyone holds the same resentment."

Calahar grunted. "When are we leaving? What are the plans?"

"I need to finish preparations," Keith said. "Then we will meet the others in the forest. Have you collected the knight and his squire? I imagine they are still tied up?"

"Yes, sir."

"Good. See that they are fed and allowed to prepare. We leave soon, and there is much work ahead."

As Calahar rode off, Keith turned to Ryker. "Before we leave, I want to take you to the armoury and the stables to ensure you are fully equipped. You will meet the man who oversees Crandrop in my absence—Old Ray. He has been here longer than almost anyone. Ray was once a young blacksmith when this village first flourished, and later became our master of weapons and horses."

As they walked through the bustling town, Keith slipped something into Ryker's pocket—a folded sheet of paper. "You need to do a better job keeping this safe," Keith said quietly.

Ryker nodded. "I will do better next time." Ryker now knew he would not be so foolish in the future. After escaping death time after time on this journey, he was starting to learn what it truly meant to lead an army.

They stopped first at a small diner. Ryker, exhausted and starving, devoured an entire meal in minutes. With his hunger satisfied, they continued on toward the armoury. The streets bustled with men receiving weapons and horses as they passed. The armoury itself appeared small from the outside, its stone istructure was humble compared to the army it supplied. Inside, the stone walls were lined with rows of weapons—swords, bows, axes, maces, and shields. Behind the counter, several sharpening wheels spun continuously. Keith led Ryker past the counter and through a wooden doorway, down a dark, winding staircase of crumbling stone steps.

The staircase opened into a large underground forge. Hot kettles of molten metal bubbled as blacksmiths hammered glowing steel into weapons. Sparks filled the air in the glow of the forge.

Keith led Ryker into a smaller chamber behind the forge. Inside, lit by candlelight, sat a thin old man with long grey hair—Old Ray—sharpening blades at a large black stone table.

"Welcome," Ray greeted them. "Keith, I hear you are heading off to war once again. I thought you swore you would never serve the Scarllend army again after they abandoned us."

"So did I," Keith replied. "But dark days are ahead, and uniting this country may be our only hope. What approaches may be worse than any army."

"Worse than the Shantrock regime?" Ray asked.

"I am not certain, but I know it will bring death to many if we do not act."

Keith continued, "I came to ask if you will oversee the town while I am gone."

"Of course," Ray said. "The forge is fully staffed, and we are producing weapons daily. I will keep the town secure."

"Excellent. For now, I need to equip Ryker with proper arms and armour."

Ray nodded and led them into a hidden storage room. As Keith snapped his fingers, rows of candles ignited across the chamber, illuminating the grand display of weapons mounted on the walls.

Gold- and silver-etched swords, shields inscribed with ancient symbols, and rare metals reflected the candlelight.

"What do you have suitable for the commander?" Keith asked.

Ray gestured to a polished silver sword mounted at chest height. "Ryker, take it."

Ryker reached for the sword. As his hand touched the hilt, a powerful surge pulsed through his arm. Confidence and strength filled him instantly.

"Magnificent," Ryker whispered.

"That blade will cut through anything on this land," Ray said. "Very few like it exist."

Keith nodded. "Now, Ray, give him the shield."

Ray removed a lightweight blue shield from the wall. "Extend your arm."

Ryker did. The shield attached effortlessly to his forearm.

"This shield will respond to your thoughts," Ray explained. "It can grow and adapt in battle, but it requires great focus and discipline. You will learn its full power if you prove worthy."

Their next stop was the stables. Ray led them through a hidden passage underground rather than forcing them to climb countless stairs again.

The three emerged inside the large stables, surrounded by strong, trained warhorses. Four magnificent stallions stood before them, their muscular frames shining under the lantern light.

"These are my best stallions," Ray announced. "You may choose one for yourself, Ryker."

Keith stepped aside. "Choose wisely, Chief."

Ryker studied the horses carefully. The first one stomped aggressively. He knew instantly it was not the one. The second was uninterested, returning to its hay.

The third—a massive black destrier, one of the greatest breeds of warhorse—locked eyes with Ryker. As Ryker approached, the horse lowered its head, allowing him to gently pat its nose.

"What is this one's story?" Ryker asked.

"A warhorse with unmatched strength and endurance," Ray replied. "He has served many, but never had a true name."

Without hesitation, Ryker said, "Shadow."

"Perfect choice," Ray nodded.

Keith smiled. "Now, let us retrieve your companions."

Keith grabbed Ryker by the shoulder and teleported them outside.

They arrived to find Derk and Calahar brawling fiercely in the middle of the town square. Both men were bloodied but refused to yield.

"ENOUGH!" Keith's booming voice echoed through the town, freezing everyone in place.

The crowd dispersed as Keith approached the two men.

"What is this about?" Keith asked firmly.

Calahar sneered. "This knight insulted our horses. I should have killed him when I had the chance!"

Derk replied, "I merely said my horse back home was stronger. That is all."

Keith stepped between them. "That is enough. Calahar, rally the troops. Ray, prepare Derk and the squire with proper weapons, armour, and horses. We leave within the hour."

The entire town buzzed with activity.

Ray armed Sir Derk and Squire Billy with sharpened blades,

stiff armour, and fresh mounts.

Keith and Ryker, meanwhile, spread word to the rest of the town, finalizing their strategy in private. They decided to avoid the underground tunnels, travelling directly across the land to free villages along the way, striking at the enemy's strongholds as they advanced toward the castle gates.

After an hour, Keith and Ryker stood beneath a towering statue in the town square, addressing over a thousand men and horses gathered before them.

Keith raised his voice to the crowd.

"You stand here today not for the king or the knights, but for the people of this land who have suffered under King Diablo's wrath. The only way to save Scarllend is to unite and strike back. Today, we march to reclaim our home, our kingdom, and our freedom. The fate of this land depends on us."

"I am Commander Ryker. I thank you all on behalf of myself, the kingdom, and everyone in the nation who struggles and is in danger. Your people are experts at rallying together—and this is what the nation needs: warriors with your resilience." Ryker realized he was truly a commander, fighting alongside ancient warriors like the elves, gnomes, and Keith's people, who had placed their trust in him.

After Ryker's moving speech, Keith reared his horse onto its hind legs, letting out a sharp call before riding forward.

Calahar and Ryker followed closely behind, the warriors of Crandrop marching proudly after them. Together, they rode toward the forest to join forces with the elves, the gnomes, and the pixies—for the battle that would determine Scarllend's fate.

CHAPTER 15

After a long hike through the woods led by Keith and Ryker, they finally arrived at the heart of the forest. It was a massive central clearing where all the forest's trails and creeks intersected, forming a wide open space with a quiet pond and several large trees. At first glance, it appeared that they were the only ones there—but then, movement began.

Elves quietly peeked through the trees. Gnomes popped out from the treetops, many riding birds and swooping down gracefully. Several pixies fluttered forward to take their places at the front.

Ronco, King of the Gnomes, flew down on his great winged companion, jumped off, and grew to a larger size. Then, with a soft shimmer, Siamac, Lord of the Elves, materialized behind Keith and the other leaders.

The clearing quickly filled—horse after horse, row after row, shoulder to shoulder. Each pathway leading into the space became crowded with soldiers and magical creatures from every corner of the forest. Elves lined the woods, gnomes floated in the sky above, and pixies hovered like colourful sparks of light.

Miss Tiffany flew down and joined the front line with Thali, Dominus, and other pixies. Jason and Don climbed down from the trees where they had waited with Ronco. They could not fly like the gnomes or pixies, so they had perched in the branches until it was safe to join. Everyone had been waiting in quiet and secret.

Once everyone had emerged from hiding, all eyes turned to Keith, who stood in the center alongside Ryker, Siamac, and Ronco. Miss Tiffany fluttered just above them. At their side stood Sir Derk, Squire Billy, Calahar, Jason, and Don—leaders of the coalition to free and reunite the land of Scarllend. Siamac raised his voice, powerful and clear across the clearing.

"I thank you all for gathering today. You stand not for comfort or glory, but for the survival of our land. A great battle lies ahead, and when that battle is won, even greater challenges will remain."

"The coalition assembled here today is no longer a scattered force—you are the shield of Scarllend. United, we stand against the rising threat of Shantrock, their allies, the orcs, the ogres, and any dark powers they wield."

He paused, letting the gravity of his words settle.

"We do not fight for King Francis. We fight for Scarllend itself, for the legacy of Daniel Sable—the man who once freed this land nearly a thousand years ago. Our loyalty is to the people, to the forests, and to the future."

He took a puff from the pipe he always held nearby and exhaled a large cloud of green smoke.

"Daniel Sable united the beings of these parts when we needed it—when similar powers once overtook this entire land."

He gestured toward Ronco.

"Thanks to the wisdom of King Ronco of the Gnomes, we will begin this journey not with a long march, but with speed and stealth. Before we set off, I would like you to recognize the commander of this great nation's army."

As soon as Siamac finished speaking, Ryker let out a shout in a commanding tone:

"Your elders of the forest are very wise. Without them, my mission would have been hopeless. They will help me lead this army to greatness. With every single one of us working as a team, we will look out for each other and never give up on ourselves or the battle. You may feel beaten or even scared—yes, orcs are vicious monstrosities. But remember: we are all in this together, and we will never surrender to monsters like them or the rogue knights of Shantrock. Our hearts are in this fight, and that will make all the difference."

Ronco let out a sharp whistle.

A great flock of birds soared across the sky in a stunning synchronized display. Leading them was a massive griffin, its wings stretched wide. The great beast had the mane and fangs of a lion, a sharp beak, powerful claws, and a beautiful red-feathered wingspan. It was followed by four monstrous black condors in a perfect V formation. Behind them flew eagles, hawks, and smaller birds in thick waves, blanketing the sky.

With a burst of energy, Ronco leapt high into the air, raising his golden scepter. Slamming it into the earth, a blinding flash of magic spread across the gathering. One by one, every soldier, horse, and leader shrank to miniature size. Siamac, unaffected by the spell, remained towering above the tiny army. "Stand with your fellow troops that you arrived with," Siamac instructed, his voice still calm. "The gnomes will guide you onto the condors and eagles by your ranks. Your mounts will be secured to saddles and harnesses on the magnificent creatures you board. Though the journey is long, we must fly quickly into battle—and remain cautious."

As Ronco worked his magic, gnomes moved quickly into formation, assigning soldiers and horses to their assigned birds. Each gnome expertly handled the harnessing of the miniaturized troops and their animals. Once everything was settled, Siamac shrunk himself down as well.

The leaders—Siamac, Ronco, Keith, and Ryker—rode at the front aboard the mighty griffin. With them were Calahar, Sir Derk, Squire Billy, Jason, and Don. Siamac's top elven warriors, Malc and Angus, also joined them, renowned as the finest archers in the forest.

Miss Tiffany flew ahead of them on her own, using her natural flight and incredible speed to match the griffin's pace, fluttering in a blur of emerald and gold.

Behind them, birds carried the rest of the coalition. The highest-ranking soldiers rode the condors, while gnomes piloted squads aboard eagles, hawks, blue jays, cardinals, and robins. The pixies, though powerful in their own right, required hummingbirds to maintain the long flight—except for Tiffany, whose stamina was unmatched.

In their miniature state, no soldier required mushrooms to maintain their size. Ronco, riding at the lead, channeled his magic to keep the entire army small and weightless for the flight's duration.

The final whistles from the gnomes signaled readiness. Ronco shouted, "We are off!"

With a great heave, the griffin spread its wings and lifted into the sky, followed swiftly by the condors and the rest of the flock. The trees shrank beneath them as the sky filled with hundreds of airborne warriors, heading straight toward the kingdom's gates—and into the war that would determine Scarllend's future.

Ryker looked behind him and saw the army he had risked his life to unite. Seeing all the troops he had rallied made it feel real—he was truly fighting for something. He thought of his good friend Shorpal, who had been stricken down at the gates. He wanted to make him proud by freeing the people of the castle—and at the same time, he did not want to meet the same fate.

CHAPTER 16

here was a swampland outside of the forest where the ogres were gathering—some coming from other swamps, others from within the forest, and even a few migrating down from the East Mountains. Their leader, Big Gor, an ally of the dark lord Diablo, had summoned every ogre who could make the journey to this marshland to prepare for an assault on the forest.

Big Gor paced along the swamp's edge, watching as his troops arrived in groups. He had heard rumours that the defenders of the forest had abandoned their posts to join the army of Crandrop. Now, as he looked to the sky and saw a massive flight of birds leaving the forest, his suspicion was confirmed.

Without waiting to form a proper plan, Big Gor bellowed, "The forest is empty! The magic folk are gone! This is our chance—pillage it all! Move now!"

His monsters roared in reply. With no strategy beyond destruction, the ogres surged out of the swamp and into the woods.

At first, they smashed through the trees with ease, clubbing anything in sight and eager for prey. But the forest offered no resistance—no animals or creatures dared to show themselves. The locals were much smarter than the ogres and had gone into hiding.

Frustrated by the lack of victims, the ogres turned their rage on the forest itself. They slammed into trees with their massive bodies, knocked over trunks with brute force, and bashed everything they saw.

But the forest was not without defenders. The owls, messengers of the centaurs, took to the skies to alert the remaining warriors.

The first response came swiftly: giant hornets descended from the treetops. These were no ordinary insects—they carried massive stingers capable of piercing straight through an ogre's chest. Several ogres were taken down instantly, screaming as they collapsed.

Some ogres swung their clubs and struck the hornets mid-flight, but for each insect they swatted, more arrived in their place. The buzzing cloud swirled through the battlefield, driving the ogres into confusion.

Then came the second wave: grizzly bears.

Dozens of them charged through the woods, teeth bared and claws extended. Some leapt onto the ogres and mauled them. Others engaged in fierce grapples—ogres swinging clubs, bears snapping jaws. It was a brutal and bloody clash.

The hornets and bears gained ground at first, but soon more ogres emerged from the swamp. Their growing numbers began to overwhelm the forest's defenders. The hornets struggled to pierce through the thicker waves of ogres, and the grizzlies began to fall back under the pressure.

Now, the pillaging truly began. The ogres pushed deeper into the woods, destroying everything they could. Trees fell, shrubs were crushed, and the forest floor shook beneath their feet.

But Big Gor had made a mistake.

In his arrogance, he had forgotten about the centaurs.

The owls reached the centaur camp swiftly. Their mighty leader, Butch, was notified and wasted no time. He spread word across the forest, dispatching warriors to lock down the borders and prepare for battle.

By the hour's end, the centaur army was in motion. Butch, clad in black armour, raised his gleaming sword as he arrived at the swamp's edge. "Drive them from our forest!" he roared.

The centaurs charged. Hooves thundered across the ground, spears aimed forward, blades flashing in the dappled light. The ogres at the front barely had time to raise their clubs before they were struck down. One after another, ogres fell—arms sliced off, heads rolling, bodies crumpling beneath the charge.

The survivors turned to flee.

But the centaurs were faster.

Galloping alongside them, they cut down the ogres in retreat. Archers fired from behind, arrows piercing their backs before they could vanish into the swamp.

The once-mighty war party was shattered. The forest stood strong.

Only a handful of ogres escaped—including Big Gor. Bloodied and furious, he limped through the muck with three of his strongest warriors.

"Back to the deep swamps," Big Gor growled. "Hide until the lords call for us again."

The others nodded. "But what about you, Gor?"

"I must report to the dark lords. Diablo will hear of this failure—from me. And when we return, it will be with vengeance."

With that, the battered ogres disappeared into the shadows, their pride wounded, but their hatred still alive.

CHAPTER 17

he new recruits of Scarllend flew onward for days. Thanks to the gnomes' magic mushrooms, the birds remained strong and replenished, flying through the night without rest.

Their journey carried them over the breathtaking landscapes of Scarllend—lush forests, towering mountains, and wide valleys untouched by the devastation of war. They flew along the outer edge of the mountains, the wind howling in their ears.

At the front of the mighty griffin rode the coalition's leaders: Ronco, Siamac, Jason, Don, and the elven brothers Malc and Angus. They sat in formation, intentionally keeping their distance from Miss Tiffany.

Ryker rode alone, lost in thought for much of the journey. The magnitude of what lay ahead weighed on his mind. He looked down at the world below, heart burning with determination to protect it from the spreading evil.

He thought of the child his wife would soon bear—he was not just fighting for his people, but for the world that child would inherit.

The wind blew through his hair, carrying his solemn thoughts, until Miss Tiffany fluttered over and landed beside him. She leaned in with a sweet smile.

"Hello, handsome," she purred, twirling her hair around her finger.

Ryker gave her a puzzled look. "Hi there."

"I do not believe we have been properly introduced," she said, her voice airy and light. "My name is Tiffany. But you may call me Miss Tiffany. I must say, we have waited a long time for a saviour like you. You are far better company than those old fools over there." She gestured toward Ronco and the others.

Catching Ronco's glance, she quickly added with a giggle, "Well, I should get some air."

With a flutter of wings and a sprinkle of pixie dust, she flew off, leaving Ryker slightly dazed. She kept her distance, not wanting to raise Ronco's suspicion just yet. But in her brief exchange with Ryker, she sensed something—power, a kind of strength or knowledge she was determined to uncover.

After two long days, the army reached the outskirts of Scarllend's great kingdom. In the distance, castle walls stretched across the mountains, separating the kingdom from the lands beyond.

Flying overhead, they saw the full scale of the kingdom—soaring towers, vast courtyards, and endless buildings glittering under the morning light. Soldiers below stopped what they were doing, staring in awe as the sky filled with birds and warriors.

From the highest tower, King Francis Sable watched in disbelief.

He had feared Ryker was lost. But as he looked up at the sky flooded with warriors on the backs of birds, he knew his Commander-in-Chief had delivered beyond expectation. Ronco led the griffin into a steep dive, the other birds following close behind. As they neared the battlefield, he raised his golden scepter and slammed it into the air. A brilliant flash of light burst from the tip, restoring every soldier to full size as they leapt from their birds and landed in perfect fighting formations.

The gnomes stayed airborne, circling above to rain magic from the sky.

Below, the Shantrock army was already closing in on the castle gates. Scarllend's remaining knights held the line, but only barely. Ryker's reinforcements had arrived just in time.

The coalition forces landed between the gate and the enemy's forward ranks. For a moment, an eerie silence fell over the battlefield. The orcs and knights of Shantrock froze, stunned by the sudden arrival of an army that had fallen from the sky.

Then chaos erupted.

Siamac and Keith unleashed powerful spells—waves of red and green energy surged forward, stunning and paralyzing the front lines. Though their magic could not reach deep into the valley, their opening strike gave Scarllend's forces a vital edge.

Ryker, leading the charge, let out a thunderous battle cry.

Both sides collided in a deafening crash of steel and fury. The orcs roared, swinging massive axes, while the knights of Shantrock fought with brutal precision. The ground quaked beneath their feet.

Though more enemies poured in from the valley, Scarllend's coalition held firm. The clash of blades echoed through the air. Blood soaked the earth, but still the warriors pressed forward.

Despite the surprise attack, the enemy fought back hard. The strongest of their warriors tore through the ranks, cutting down recruits. Orcs, fuelled by rage, shrugged off spells and kept swinging at anything they could reach.

Keith fell back behind his lines, using mind magic to freeze enemies in place, making them easy targets for elven archers. Malc and Angus loosed arrow after arrow, felling enemies by the dozens.

Above, the gnomes dropped mushroom bombs. Some exploded with deadly force; others released choking toxins that paralyzed enemy ranks. Panic swept through Shantrock's army.

Pixies zipped overhead, scattering enchanted dust. Many enemy soldiers fell into hallucinations—some driven to madness, others taking their own lives to escape the horrors they imagined.

Ronco, riding atop the griffin, cast bolts of electricity and shrinking spells. Some foes were electrocuted on the spot; others shrank and were crushed under the feet of their own allies. The griffin clawed through enemies, lifting soldiers into the sky, setting them ablaze, and hurling their flaming bodies back into the fray.

But still, the enemy surged from the valley—crazed, bloodthirsty, and determined to bring Ryker's army down.

Ryker fought with General Derk at his side. They protected each other, moving in sync. When a brutal orc's axe came down on Derk, Ryker's shield suddenly moved on its own, blocking the blow. Their young squire leapt forward, stabbing the orc in the neck. Ryker finished it with a mighty swing of his blade.

As the battle reached its peak, Scarllend's remaining knights stormed out from the gates and joined the fight. With their reinforcements behind them, they pushed the enemy back toward the valley. Though the orcs and rogue knights were being defeated, they continued to take lives with every breath.

Even with the advantage of surprise, numbers, and magic, Scarllend suffered dearly. Elves fell. Gnomes were struck down and turned to mushrooms. Brave men of Crandrop were cut down beside Scarllend's knights.

The brutal struggle seemed endless—until the enemy, battered and surrounded, formed a final circle of defence. It was the last stand of Shantrock's assault.

And then, it was over.

The gates were safe. The castle was free. Scarllend had taken one great step toward wholeness.

Ronco swooped down on his griffin, grinning. "The valley is clear of vermin!" he called out triumphantly.

Siamac raised his staff to the sky, channelling the sun's power. He slammed it into the ground, unleashing a wave of brilliant light. The fallen—friend and foe—were absorbed into the earth, returning to nature.

Green grass spread across the battlefield. Trees grew. Flowers bloomed. The marble steps to the castle gleamed once more, as if the land itself was reborn.

Ryker stood in awe. He had never imagined such beauty—or such magic—could still exist in Scarllend. He had fought his first true battle as a commander. And he could feel it now—he was becoming the leader his country needed.

The castle gates opened, and King Francis stepped out, flanked by his knights. Siamac used his magic to part the crowd, clearing a path for the leaders to meet.

"Ryker," the king said with a smile, "you have outdone yourself. I was right to appoint you Commander-in-Chief. You have returned with the most incredible force I could have dreamed."

He turned to the other leaders. "And to all of you—thank you. You have brought hope back to Scarllend. For your deeds, I invite you inside for a grand feast."

"I did not come here for any damn feast," Calahar growled, spitting on the ground. "I came to fight—and to keep fighting. There is still a nation to save."

The others exchanged knowing glances. Keith laughed. "Calahar, we will fight again soon. But first, we need rest. We have not eaten properly in days."

Calahar grunted but agreed.

Keith turned to the army and raised his booming voice. "Everyone who survived this battle—come! The king has prepared a feast fit for royalty, and you have earned it!"

The leaders stepped through the gates, the army following. For many, it was their first time inside the castle. They marvelled at the towering walls, the glittering halls, the grand courtyards.

Knights lined the halls, guiding them toward the celebration —a feast not just for food, but for victory, unity, and the dream of a free Scarllend.

CHAPTER 18

Big Gor had made the long journey back to Shantrock Castle, where he would face the powerful leaders of the evil alliance. He dreaded what awaited him—the shame of failure and the fury of his masters.

Shantrock Castle stood beneath jagged mountains in the east, where many creatures loyal to Diablo lurked. The land around it was barren: a dead valley of twisted trees, cracked earth, and withered shrubs. The castle itself was a fraction of Scarllend's size. Four small towers sat at its corners, with a crumbling central tower in the middle. The walls, built from filthy, rotting brick, oozed decay. Orcs and knights patrolled the battlements in eerie silence.

Once a fortress guarding against the mountain creatures, it was now ruled by them—a rotting monument to its cursed history.

Big Gor lumbered toward the main gate. The guards stepped aside without a word, letting him pass. Inside the gloomy courtyard, the people looked lifeless—gaunt faces and hollow eyes. The kingdom felt more like a prison for the damned.

He climbed the castle's winding staircase, dimly lit by flickering candles, until he reached the highest quarters where Diablo and the other dark lords schemed.

At the top, a thick steel door blocked his path. He knocked heavily.

A growling voice answered from within. "Come in."

The lock clicked.

Big Gor pushed the door open slowly. The room was small, but suffocating with tension. Inside sat three of the most feared beings in all of Scarllend. The silence was unbearable. Big Gor's heart pounded like a war drum.

To the right sat Diablo, self-proclaimed king of Shantrock. His fiery red hair spilled from beneath a twisted iron crown. His thick beard was streaked with ash, and his eyes burned with equal parts madness and fear.

To the left sat Orkin, a monstrous orc commander clad in heavy iron armour. His visor ran down the bridge of his nose, hiding a mouth of jagged fangs. Black hair flowed down his back, and his cracked, scarred skin looked like shattered stone.

At the head of the table stood Blitzker—the leader of the volcanic realm. His black robes rippled with living flame. Fire licked up his arms and shoulders, pulsing with each breath. The blaze atop his hood hissed with life.

Blitzker turned slowly to face Big Gor. His voice was sharp and cold.

"So... what news do you bring, ogre? And remember—I know

lies when I hear them."

Big Gor swallowed and tried to speak with composure.

"Well, boss... it did not go exactly as planned."

Blitzker's eyes narrowed.

"That does not surprise me. You have proven poor at planning. Now sit. Explain your failure—clearly."

Big Gor dropped into a chair, sweat beading on his brow.

"We set up the meeting point, just like you said. But... the centaurs came before we could do much."

Blitzker's voice cut like ice.

"Is that because they found you—or because you attacked before you were supposed to?"

Big Gor stammered.

"No, boss! We stayed hidden. But when the birds flew out of the forest—with men riding them—we figured the forest was empty. It looked like the perfect time to strike."

Blitzker's fire hissed and crackled.

"Thank you for confirming my suspicion."

He stepped closer, voice dropping to a chilling whisper.

"So... your brilliant plan was to attack without orders because it 'looked like a good time'?"

Big Gor trembled.

"It seemed like the perfect opportunity. I thought... I thought of what a great leader like yourself would do!"

Blitzker stared him down.

"And tell me—what do you think someone as great and powerful as myself would do in this situation?"

Big Gor's chest tightened. He could hardly breathe. Even the other lords in the room shifted uneasily, almost pitying the doomed ogre.

After a long pause, Big Gor finally stuttered,

"I... I think you'd give me a second chance to make a better plan and try again."

Blitzker's eyes flared.

"You are simply too foolish to serve me any longer."

His flaming hand landed heavily on Big Gor's shoulder. In seconds, the ogre's body was engulfed in fire, reduced to ash, the chair scorched and smouldering beneath the pile.

Diablo and Orkin flinched, terror tightening in their chests. Diablo's hand drifted to his throat.

Blitzker turned his burning gaze to Orkin.

"You will now lead both your orcs and what remains of the ogres. March on Crandrop while it is vulnerable. Leave the forest alone. Your goal is simple—burn Crandrop to the ground."

Orkin nodded, grim and silent.

Blitzker then turned on Diablo. The king of Shantrock visibly shook, sweat dripping down his face.

"You... you gave up the gate!" Blitzker roared.

His voice turned to a scream of fury, echoing like thunder.

"But... I will give you one final chance."

He lunged and grabbed Diablo by the throat, lifting him into the air.

"There is still something I require," he hissed.

"The key to releasing my people. The map still exists—I can feel it. Someone at that castle holds it."

Diablo gasped, his skin blistering beneath Blitzker's fiery grip.

"Y-yes, sir..." he choked.

Blitzker hurled him across the room. Diablo crashed into the stone wall and crumpled to the floor, barely conscious.

"You will gather the leprechauns—the few who still serve you

—and send them to retrieve the map. If you fail again... your fate will be worse than his."

He pointed to the pile of Big Gor's ashes.

Blitzker turned back to Orkin.

"While Diablo chases my map, you will keep Scarllend from regaining ground. Strike hard. No mercy."

With that, Blitzker erupted into a column of fire and vanished.

Orkin left the room silently.

Diablo lay slumped against the wall, his face burned, feverish sweat soaking his robes. His mind raced.

He had to find the leprechauns—the very ones he had betrayed with false promises of gold and glory. The few that survived now lived in isolation, far from the world of men. And now, he would have to crawl back to them—a desperate king on the edge of ruin.

CHAPTER 19

ehind the walls of Scarllend Castle, a grand victory was being celebrated. But for the leaders of the coalition, the mood was far from festive. Keith and the others were eager to focus on planning their next move with Ryker and the king.

King Sable, however, insisted that a feast be held first—a grand banquet to commemorate reclaiming the gate. It was his way of showing gratitude.

They met briefly with the king while preparations were underway. Keith, Ryker, Siamac, Ronco, and Miss Tiffany gathered with him in his quarters to discuss immediate plans. A large number of troops remained stationed outside the gate, guarding against any sudden reinforcements from Shantrock.

The king thanked them sincerely.

"Your help is greatly appreciated," he said. "And Ryker, you outdid yourself bringing these great soldiers and their armies. I was not even sure if gnomes and elves still existed—it has been so long since they served with us."

"I guess that tells you how long it has been since you forgot about us all," Ronco replied sharply.

King Sable looked stunned.

Keith added, "Do not act surprised. Did you forget about pulling your entire army out of the forest when your precious gates were threatened?"

"I am truly sorry for the decisions made in the past," the king admitted. "I was new to the throne and did not understand proper strategy. That is why I want to thank you, reward you with one of the greatest meals you have ever had, and knight you all as members of our army."

"We do not need your thanks," Keith replied coolly. "We did not come here to protect you. We came to unite the armies because you were incapable of freeing your own castle without us.

Frankly, I had hoped your backbone was stronger—like your ancestor. But all you seem concerned about is your dinner."

The king was taken aback by Keith's bluntness.

Keith continued, "I suggest you let us work directly with Ryker. Give him full control of your army. From what I have seen, your Commander-in-Chief shows far more competence."

"I do not appreciate your tone," King Francis said stiffly.

"But I admit you are right about one thing. I trust Ryker's leadership. Still, I believe our men deserve rest and morale after the battle. The feast will proceed, and we will rotate troops outside the gates in shifts."

Keith relented.

"Fine. A night's rest will serve everyone. Tomorrow, we strategize. But your kitchen better know how to cook, or you will have angry soldiers on your hands."

Fortunately, the king's kitchen staff had been trained for generations, passing knowledge down through their elders. Inside Scarllend Castle, many working-class citizens served in essential roles—from cleaning and cooking to horse training and knighthood.

By the time the council ended, the banquet hall was nearly full—especially the tables reserved for higher-ranking members of the newly united army. Knights helped escort citizens to their seats, avoiding chaos.

Within the hour, the grand hall brimmed with energy. Warm roasted meats, spiced cider, and polished silverware glinted beneath the glow of dozens of chandeliers.

The king entered with Queen Emily and Princess Delilah, walking proudly down the central aisle. As they approached the stage, Queen Emily caught sight of someone familiar—Don. Their eyes met. A brief, knowing smile passed between them.

King Francis, slightly unsettled, nudged his wife to keep moving.

Once on stage, the king delivered a heartfelt speech, thanking everyone—from knights to kitchen staff—for their service. He introduced the new coalition leaders and assured the people that everyone in the kingdom would be trained for war.

"Enjoy this evening," he said.

"Celebrate—for tomorrow begins the long road ahead. A road straight toward Shantrock."

After speaking, the royal family retired briefly to a private dining room.

Later, they returned to mingle with the soldiers. As the king chatted with a group of gnomes about Scarllend's history, Queen

Emily noticed Don, Jason, and Ronco at another table. She approached with a smile.

"Well, is that really who I think it is?" she said warmly.

Don looked up, then smiled.

"It has been a long time. I thought you would have forgotten me by now."

"Could never forget you. You were one of the bravest knights I ever knew. After your platoon pulled back, I never heard more about you. I assumed you were dead."

"Well, here I am—alive and kicking after all these years."

They shared a few stories of old times. Don introduced Jason, who gave the Queen a polite wave and explained how they had joined Ryker's mission.

While the king remained distracted, Princess Delilah quietly joined her mother. When introduced to Jason, he stood and shook her hand. The moment their hands touched, he felt something—a powerful spark, as though his heart had caught fire.

"Well, hello," Jason said nervously.

"It is an honour to meet you, Princess."

Delilah blushed lightly and smiled.

"And I am grateful for brave men like you, fighting for our kingdom."

"You are very welcome," Jason replied with a grin.

"It is an honour to serve both of you fine ladies."

As Queen Emily led Delilah back toward the king, Delilah turned briefly, offering Jason a sweet smile and wave. He stood frozen, completely enchanted.

"You two are damn lucky," Ronco chuckled, puffing green and red smoke from his pipe.

"Royalty like that does not smile at just anyone."

Don shrugged.

"We knew each other growing up. But she chose royalty long ago."

"Well, you are back now," Ronco smirked.

"Maybe fate is giving you both another shot."

They clinked their mugs and laughed heartily.

Not everyone was amused.

From a few tables away, Miss Tiffany watched the exchange with simmering jealousy. She ducked beneath a table, glaring as the princess spoke with Don and Jason. She was already scheming ways to sabotage them. But for now, her attention shifted.

She was curious about Ryker.

Despite her powers, she had not yet spent much time with him—and unlike others, she could not easily read him. That alone frustrated her.

Miss Tiffany slipped out of the banquet hall, flying quietly through the castle's corridors. Using her ability to sense emotions, she honed in on a strong, steady energy that pulled her up a spiralling stairwell.

At the top, she found a dim hallway where soft voices echoed.

It was Ryker and his wife.

His wife's voice trembled as she confessed her fears—that she might lose him in the war, that their child might grow up without a father.

Ryker embraced her gently.

"I promise you, I will return," he whispered.

"I want our child to grow up in a free kingdom. And I will do everything I must to make sure that happens. But sacrifices will be required—just not ours."

Tears streamed down her face as she clung to him.

Miss Tiffany lingered in the shadows, watching. She could feel his emotional conflict—but also sensed something deeper. Something powerful. Something she could not quite grasp. That unsettled her more than she liked to admit.

She narrowed her eyes.

For now, she would leave him be. But she was determined to figure him out. And soon.

The next couple of days at the castle were spent training, sorting the platoons, and appointing the right soldiers to the right squads. Many had already been dispersed around the valley, guarding a border where an attack was much expected. The rest of the soldiers remained in the castle, meeting with the rest of the army. They had a one-week training plan, though troops would be disbursed before that time.

On the first day of training, a meeting was held where all members of the army gathered around the middle courtyard and scattered across the castle. The king attended, speaking from the roof of a small tower used as a stage. He spoke as loudly as he could, but his voice was weak and barely carried across the courtyard. The soldiers strained to hear him—some leaning forward, others muttering quietly.

He said his words anyway and recognized Ryker as the Grand Commander-in-Chief of the army. As Ryker stepped forward to address the crowd, a great roar of cheers erupted—the soldiers trusted him. His voice carried strong, bold, and filled with command.

Ryker spoke boldly, announcing the rest of the new ranks. Keith, Lord Siamac, King Ronco, and Miss Tiffany were announced as grand officers, and each was allowed to appoint their own generals. Ronco appointed Jason and Don. Siamac chose the two great archers, Malc and Angus. Keith, of course, went with Calahar. Ryker made his own choice, selecting his great new companion Derk. Derk's chest swelled with pride as his name was called. Ryker also declared Squire Billy a full-fledged knight after the bravery he had shown along their wild adventures. Billy beamed with joy, gripping his new sword tightly.

During the days of training, experienced knights were sent out to the perimeter of the castle. They had strengthened their border in just a few days. Many of the trainees were young squires heading into battle for the first time; some had never even left the castle before. Civilians from nearby towns had also come to train. Not many showed up, but they claimed many more were willing to fight—only Shantrock had moved so far into their region that few were free to come. Still, it sounded as though they would have backup in every place they went.

Throughout the training days, Jason and Don were getting quite friendly with the royalty. Princess Delilah followed Jason everywhere he went and made a point of sitting beside him when he would take a break and light a herbal cigar. Whenever she arrived, Jason's heart raced, and the other soldiers teased him with knowing grins. Jason caught wise to this and told Ronco and his father to leave him be.

As Don would go somewhere else to have a smoke, the queen

would pop out of nowhere and find him. She was more discreet, telling him to come sit around the corner. She would smoke with him, never bumming a cigar—she always brought her own. The king did not know that she smoked, nor about any of what was going on. He had the elders Ronco and Siamac chatting his ear off, telling him about his family's history and how his ancestors had brought peace to the nation for hundreds of years, until the conflict between two brothers began the war that escalated into what it was today.

With just a day left in training, most of the army had strengthened the border and were waiting for Ryker and the other leaders to meet them in the valley and head their way after finalizing platoons.

As the leaders gathered and formed their plans, Keith started getting a very uneasy feeling in his heart—a pain in his side, his chest tightening, breath shortening, and a strong energy weighing on him. His vision blurred and his knees weakened.

The orcs had made their way across the far east mountains near Shantrock, where they now called home. They were slowly approaching the horizon of Crandrop, still a long way away. But they could see the town and knew they were on the right path.

The fiery Lord Blitzker had supplied Orkin and his men with giant chunks of volcanic rock that he had retrieved from atop his volcanic mountain. His strong powers allowed him to immerse into the lava and heave the mighty boulders out. The rocks were loaded into catapults made with solid iron to keep them from burning during travel.

As they neared closer, they debated when to take their shots—then let loose on the town. They all carried torches along with their weapons.

Eventually, they reached a hilltop that stood just above the town of Crandrop. Orkin's top man, The General, led the attack and halted the orcs and ogres beside him. He made the decision to drop the bombs. The catapults fired large chunks of volcanic rock across the sky, raining down upon the unsuspecting town.

For the townspeople of Crandrop, it was just another peaceful day until one of the few guards noticed the orcs approaching and alerted Ray and the rest of the town. Ray called for a party to clear them out. As the town began to prepare for battle, the large burning rocks came crashing down. Several flew in a V formation, slamming into buildings.

The soldiers who were rallying scattered as the bombs rained down. One smashed into a large building behind them, the wooden structure exploding as flames swept through the town. This was just one of many to hit. The town was in disarray.

Ray jumped on his horse and gathered everyone he could. He and three other Crandrop soldiers ran through the burning town, checking everywhere for survivors. They found some hiding in half-burnt buildings; others managed to reach personal bomb shelters. Ray brought everyone he could find to the town bunker.

The survivors made their way from the cellars to the underground tunnel system. Very few survived, but the few dozen who did arrived in a panic. Ray got everyone willing to fight ready to move to the hilltops. Twenty men were prepared to take on whatever had started this attack.

But Ray suddenly froze. A cold dread swept through him. A vision came—flames swirling into a giant vortex, Keith's unhooded face flashing in the fire. His chest tightened in terror. Before he could leave his post, he heard a word echo in his mind:

"Halt."

As he waited at the bunker, monsters crashed through the town, destroying everything. But they found no survivors—they were all hidden. Once the orcs and ogres finished their destruction, they set their sights on the forest.

Back at Scarllend Castle, Keith collapsed to his knees, hand on his chest, witnessing all this horror firsthand. His eyes glowed faintly as he sent his consciousness to Crandrop, merging his vision with the fire.

He rose, floating two feet in the air, his hood down revealing his awful face to all. The room gasped in horror. A fiery storm swirled around him. Keith became one with the fire, attaching himself to every enemy—and burning them alive until they were nothing but ash. Once every vile creature was dead, he gathered the flames into a massive blast that burned itself out completely.

The town was in ruins. Nothing looked the same. Buildings collapsed into blackened rubble. Ray sensed the horror had passed and went with a few soldiers to investigate. They fell to their knees at the devastation.

Keith, who had remained floating, now dropped to the ground, gasping for air. He was weak, barely staying conscious.

"We should not have come here," Keith rasped. "How could I be so foolish to leave our post?" Then he begged for air.

Calahar came running and yelled, "Get him off the ground!" Then he grabbed him with another man from Crandrop.

"Calahar, we should not have come here. We must go back now to Crandrop. It's an awful scene," Keith whimpered, then let out a horrid scream.

"I would love to leave right now, but you need your rest, sir,"

Calahar said. He turned to the others and yelled, "Let's get him a bed now!"

They took him to the closest spare room and laid him down as he coughed up black phlegm.

"The town has been destroyed. The orcs must pay for what they have done. The forest is now vulnerable," Keith gasped. "We'll need to send a party there and regroup with the survivors. I feel Ray's presence—he is still alive, with others. They need guidance."

Keith continued weakly, "I will talk to the others and negotiate who will come with us. I foresee we may even need the giants' help, though it will not be easy to reach them across the mountains."

"We will leave as soon as you get your rest in."

"Yes. Get everyone prepared. I will tell them all when I awake." Then Keith faded into sleep in a split second.

Calahar was furious inside. He bottled up his rage, gave instructions for preparations, and left the room. As he walked out, lighting a cigarette, he nearly bumped into Ryker.

Calahar took a long drag and blew smoke into Ryker's face. Ryker coughed and said calmly, "I have let everyone know. The council is deciding who is going where. Final approval will come from Keith."

"Well, I do not care where the hell you guys go. I'm going back to Crandrop and that's that."

"I do not care where you are going either. Just letting you know so you will be ready."

"I'm always ready," Calahar growled, blowing more smoke into Ryker's face and walking away.

The army started preparing. Ryker told his wife they were

leaving again, and the evening was emotional and heartfelt. Since it was their last night, the Princess and Jason spent the evening walking through the castle courtyards, stealing private moments. They found a quiet, unused tower and slumbered there for the night.

The queen, too, continued her secret meetings with Don, the old flame rekindled in the shadows.

Though they thought they were in secret, three tricky pixies hovered nearby, letting little slip past them.

Ryker had much weighing on him but chose to spend his last evening by his wife's side, his hand resting gently on her stomach, feeling the future growing inside her—scared for the battles to come and what the future might hold.

CHAPTER 21

n the other side of Scarllend, inside the dark towers of the Shantrock castle, the evil lord Diablo scrambled to gather his belongings for a secret journey. He was heading deep into the darkest parts of the forest—far beyond the reach of elves, gnomes, pixies, or centaurs. He was going to where he had banished the leprechauns long ago, after sending them into a war they could never win.

The leprechauns had once warred with many throughout the forest, but none more than the gnomes. After centuries of stale battles and dwindling numbers, Diablo approached them with an offer. He promised them land, power, and leadership if they would attack deep into the forest. The leprechauns, desperate, accepted. With their cunning magic, they struck first and seized large portions of land by surprise.

But Diablo had never intended to truly aid them. Once the others of the forest organized their defense, he quickly abandoned the leprechauns and sent his orcs to destroy their homes and slaughter those who returned. The few who survived lived in quiet exile, unknown to most—except Diablo. He had kept their location hidden, knowing one day they might still serve his needs.

Now that day had come.

As Diablo hurried through his castle preparing for his journey, he knew Blitzker had ordered him to retrieve the map. But Diablo also had his own demands to make of the leprechauns.

Meanwhile, far beneath the earth in Volcanica, Blitzker stood upon his balcony high above a pool of lava. His volcanic kingdom—a land of jagged stone and rivers of fire—churned with heat and power. Below him, his fiery minions were building yet another monument to their master, only to destroy it again for the sake of rebuilding—an endless cycle of forced worship.

He had ruled them for centuries, tormenting his own people while plotting his revenge on the surface world.

The fiery Lord Blitzker felt the impact of his latest attack upon Crandrop. He knew Scarllend was growing weaker, and his time was drawing near.

Now he addressed his people.

Blitzker's voice boomed across the land like an earthquake:

"My people! Our centuries of suffering will soon pay off. For too long we have been cast into shadow—banished, forgotten, laughed at by the surface world!

But no more. Soon I will hold what I have sought for lifetimes. Soon I will rise. The earth walkers will feel the fires of our pain. And when we rise, we shall burn their world into dust! Prepare yourselves, for the day approaches. You shall give death—but be ready, for death may take you first!"

As his words echoed, he shot flames from his palms into the lava, causing great plumes of bubbling fire to rise across his volcanic kingdom. The minions cheered wildly. For once, their endless torment held a flicker of hope—hope that their long wait for freedom and vengeance was almost at hand.

Early the next morning, Keith awoke inside the Scarllend castle. Though still weakened, his strength was returning. He gathered the soldiers of Crandrop into the courtyard as he prepared to lead them home.

The leaders of the army met with him before their departure. Keith addressed them firmly.

"This is where our paths separate. Our people need us back home. But I ask one favour before we leave: if you want our help again, I need Siamac's magic of rejuvenation at my side. With our magic together, we can hold off any who come against us, and he can restore the land that has decayed. Without him, we will dedicate our lives to rebuilding what was lost."

Ryker opened his mouth to respond, but before he could speak, Siamac stepped forward.

"I will go," the elven lord said. "Your people need my powers, and we may need yours again before this war is done. I will leave Malc and Angus to serve with Ronco's platoon."

"Good boys," Ronco chuckled. "I will just have to make sure they do not get into too much trouble with Jason and Don around."

"Well, it is settled," Ryker said. "Prepare the troops. I will lead alongside General Derk and Sir Billy. We will each take a portion of the army and spread out, covering more ground."

Miss Tiffany fluttered nearby, waiting for her moment.

As Ryker spoke, she flicked her wand subtly, releasing a faint glimmer of magic into the air.

Without hesitation, Ryker's next words came out as though spoken by his own will:

"Miss Tiffany will be coming alongside me as my second-in-command."

A collective groan rippled through the ranks. Ronco's eyes narrowed immediately. His gut twisted.

That sly little witch... he thought.

Tiffany smiled sweetly at him, meeting his stare without flinching. She could sense his suspicion. As much as she looked down on the old gnome, she knew better than to underestimate him. Ronco, for all his playful grumbling, was no fool—and might become her biggest problem yet.

As the forces of Scarllend prepared to split paths, distant storms gathered across the land.

Far to the north, Diablo crept toward the hidden leprechauns. Deep beneath the earth, Blitzker's fiery army expanded, their drills pushing ever closer to the surface.

And above it all, the fragile alliance that Ryker had built stood on the edge of a coming storm—one far greater than any of them could yet imagine.

The real war was only beginning.

To be continued...

www.ingramcontent.com/pod-product-compliance
Lightning Source LLC
Chambersburg PA
CBHW010729310726
48971CB00009B/2781